AT THE END OF THE RAINBOW

Alex is escaping from an unhappy love affair. She finds employment helping Julian to finish writing his latest book. Julian is partially paralysed, and confined to a wheelchair — the result of a car accident in which his wife was killed. He could improve — perhaps even restore — his mobility by accepting new medical treatment. But he goes on punishing himself. Can Alex and Julian forget the past, and find a future together?

Books by Wendy Kremer
in the Linford Romance Library:

REAP THE WHIRLWIND

WENDY KREMER

AT THE END OF THE RAINBOW

Complete and Unabridged

LINFORD
Leicester

First published in Great Britain in 2008

First Linford Edition
published 2010

Copyright © 2008 by Wendy Kremer
All rights reserved

British Library CIP Data

Kremer, Wendy.
At the end of the rainbow. - -
(Linford romance library)
1. Traffic accident victims- -Psychology- -
Fiction. 2. Authorship- -Collaboration- -
Fiction. 3. Love stories. 4. Large type books.
I. Title II. Series
823.9'2–dc22

ISBN 978–1–44480–183–5

Published by
F. A. Thorpe (Publishing)
Anstey, Leicestershire

Set by Words & Graphics Ltd.
Anstey, Leicestershire
Printed and bound in Great Britain by
T. J. International Ltd., Padstow, Cornwall

This book is printed on acid-free paper

1

She was glad that she'd set out early enough, and managed to be roughly on time despite the unexpected hold-up on the motorway. The village, a few miles from Coniston, was a modest picturesque place and she'd found Charter House quite easily. It was the last cottage at the end of a meandering lane, near the centre of the village, and not far from the old church.

'This way, Miss Paxton.'

Alex followed Mrs Rochdale, a motherly figure enveloped in an old-fashioned wrap-around pinafore, along a panelled corridor. She waited as the older woman knocked, and pushed the door open, before standing aside. Alex smiled her thanks and unconsciously straightened her shoulders.

The study-cum-office was low-beamed with whitewashed walls. One of the small

1

upper sections of the leaded window was open; spring breezes teased at the flowered chintz curtains. Behind a large desk strewn with books and papers sat a man, his hands busy turning the pages of a thick book. Alex mused that the computer and a modern desk lamp looked slightly incongruous in these surround-ings; she shook her wandering thoughts and concentrated on the man behind the desk. As she walked towards him, he looked up and she sensed his sur-prise, but she kept going and extended a hand.

'How do you do, Professor Cordell?'

He was clearly puzzled. 'Who are you? I'm expecting Alex Paxton.'

'Yes, that's right — I'm Alex Paxton.'

Her hand was still poised halfway across the desktop; he got up with a little diffi-culty and reached forward to grasp it briefly before he put his hands on the desk to take his weight. Alex noticed some crutches lay against the edge of the desk; she kept her expression neutral and adjusted her shoulder bag to a more

2

comfortable position. A golden retriever, its tail wagging frantically, appeared. Alex bent to stroke it and stared into the dog's friendly brown eyes.

'I was expecting a man. Alex is a man's name.' His voice was curt and categorical.

She looked at him and smiled weakly. 'An understandable mistake. My name is officially Alexandra, but everyone calls me Alex.' She could see that he was nettled. 'I've done research work before, Mr Cordell, and my secretarial skills are above average, as you can see in my application. Does it make any difference whether I'm male or female?'

His dark grey eyes were guarded and almost hostile. He ran his fingers through his hair. 'This is a living-in job, and it would mean less disruption if my assistant was a man. From my point of view that is a very big difference.'

Her lids came down for a second to hide her frustration. It seemed the journey had been for nothing after all. When she glanced at him again, he was watching her with silent deliberation.

'If you want a male assistant, then there's no point in any further discussion, is there? I won't waste any more of your time.' Alex turned away towards the door, not waiting for an answer. 'Good morning, Mr Cordell. I'll find my own way out.'

Unnoticed by her, he lowered himself to his chair again and was quiet for a second as his eyes narrowed. Alex already had her hand on the door latch. 'Wait! . . . I haven't got time to go through the business of finding someone new all over again.' His fingers ran through his hair again in a gesture of slight frustration. 'The book is already behind schedule. Sit down.'

'I'll tell you roughly what the work entails, and what I expect you to do. Tell me if you can cope, or not. I need a competent assistant, someone who can work independently.' He added. 'Although I don't pretend that I would have preferred a male assistant.'

Alex returned to the desk; his words

were not the beginning she'd hoped for and she fought an inner battle not to walk straight out of the door, but at the moment she was more interested in having an interim away from her hometown than worrying about small irritations caused by unforeseen circumstances. This job had seemed heaven-sent. If Julian Cordell did turn out to be a difficult employer, she could cope with that — she had enough experience of awkward bosses. She leaned back into the chair and the dog sidled up to her; she stroked its head reassuringly.

He glanced briefly at the retriever. 'You don't mind dogs? Good! That would have been an insurmountable hurdle. Josh, don't be a nuisance, come here!' The dog obeyed immediately, his tail wagging furiously as he looked up at his master with adoring eyes.

As Julian Cordell began to describe her workload and more or less repeated the terms of employment she already remembered from the advertisement,

Alex had the opportunity to study him, and listen to his information at the same time. His black hair was cut short, and flecked with grey at the temples. His hands were beautiful, long-fingered and strong. His voice was clear and his skin had an olive tone. Either he had Mediterranean ancestors, or he spent a lot of time outdoors.

Alex guessed that he'd been going through the pros and cons of employing her and had decided to throw his prejudice overboard for the sake of progress. 'Any questions?'

Alex was too much of a professional to feel any frustration at the way the interview had gone; she was applying for a job — the advertisement should have been more explicit about the desire for a male assistant, but she grudgingly admitted now that under the circumstances his reaction was understandable.

'No, it all sounds quite straightforward. I don't envisage any difficulties.' It was up to her now to prove to him that he'd made the right decision, and she would.

'Good. When can you start?'

She noted that he didn't ask her if she wanted the job, he presumed that she did. Her hazel eyes twinkled. 'How about now?' Alex watched his reactions. That should jog him!

It did, he looked startled. 'Now? You came prepared to stay?'

'Well, I didn't exactly expect to take up residence here today, but I didn't intend to make the journey both ways all in one day either. I planned to stay overnight in the district, before travelling back tomorrow. I have a small suitcase with enough things for a couple of days. I can pick up what I need for a longer stay from home at the weekend. If every day is as important as you make it, then I ought to get started as soon as possible.'

He leaned back. For the first time Alex noticed touches of surprise and humour around his mouth and eyes. So, he was human after all!

Julian studied her more carefully; noted the high cheekbones, generous mouth, chestnut hair and creamy skin.

In a more conciliatory tone he said, 'Good! I see that you have the right attitude. Tell Mrs Rochdale you'll be staying; she'll sort out a room for you. If you really mean it, after lunch and when you've unpacked, I'll give you the first section and if you can understand my writing you can begin to put it into a readable form.'

She stood up, and cleared her throat. 'Where do I find Mrs Rochdale?'

He glanced up at the grandfather clock in the corner. 'She'll be preparing lunch in the kitchen; go along the corridor to the door at the end.' He gave her a grudging nod, and began to shuffle some papers again. He followed her with his eye as she moved with fluid strides to the door, and then turned his attention once more to the work she'd interrupted a few minutes ago.

⋆ ⋆ ⋆

'I hope you have everything you need, Miss.'

Alex viewed the tastefully arranged room decorated in shades of eggshell blue and cream, and looked briefly out of the window at the large rambling garden at the rear of the house, and beyond that to the fells in the distance. 'Oh, I'm sure I'll be comfortable; it's a lovely room. Please call me Alex.'

'I will, Miss . . . if you call me Annie. Julian only calls me Mrs Rochdale in front of strangers. I must say, it'll be pleasant to have another female in the house again. The bathroom is next door, and my room is at the end of the corridor. Julian sleeps downstairs since the accident. He had a former storeroom converted into a bathroom, and the room next door into a bedroom — it saves him climbing stairs.'

'Accident? I couldn't help noticing the crutches. What happened?'

'A car accident; over three years ago. He was in a wheelchair for a year, but has gradually improved enough to get around with crutches. Progress has come to a standstill now although Dr Arden keeps telling him another operation will improve things even more. He won't listen.' She used the corner of her apron to wipe some invisible dust from the surface of a honey coloured chest of drawers. 'I know that he has a clever brain, but I wish that he'd sometimes use it to think about himself, and how to improve his lifestyle, and not just about producing books.'

'You . . . you've known him a long time then?'

'I've been housekeeper for five years. I always lived locally. My husband died suddenly. We didn't have any children, and I had to do something to occupy my time. I came to them daily in the beginning, but after the accident I moved in. I rented out my cottage. It was easier for me, and better for him. He isn't on his own if I'm here.'

Alex nodded understandingly. 'It must have been a very difficult time. What about Mrs Cordell? I gather there was a Mrs Cordell?'

She nodded. 'Gillian? Oh, she was killed in the crash, that's what made it even more tragic. He blamed himself for what happened, and still does I think.' She looked at her watch. 'Well, I must get back to the kitchen. Lunch will be ready in half-an-hour. We eat in the kitchen; it's more practical and more comfortable all round.'

Alex smiled and Annie bustled off. She began to unpack her small case. She was glad she'd found out about the accident before she'd asked the wrong questions.

The juicy hotpot with dumplings was delicious. Alex and Julian viewed each other with neutral expressions now and then across the checked tablecloth. Annie was a chatty person by nature, and Alex was glad to find she filled any silent interludes quite naturally with news of the village she'd heard at the shop that morning. Julian nodded and made suitable comments.

Looking at them, Alex wondered how

she'd fit into this well-ordered world; at the moment it was hard to tell. Even if the job were only for five months it would be difficult if she and Julian Cordell didn't harmonise. At the end of the meal, he reached for his crutches and got up with surprising agility.

Addressing Alex before he moved towards the door, he said, 'If you still want to start this afternoon, I'll be in the office.' Alex nodded.

She tarried a little longer with Annie. 'Tell me more about the village.'

Annie Rochdale regarded Alex across the table and obliged. 'The church is very old. Some parts are supposed to be almost a thousand years old. The village was mentioned in the Doomsday Book. The centre of the village is under one of those order things; it can't be altered. Julian knows all about its history, if you're interested ask him. People are generally friendly, and if you make an effort you'll soon feel at home.'.

Annie liked the girl's open face, with its creamy skin and sprinkling of freckles. She was slim but not skinny and she'd enjoyed the meal, so she didn't count calories. At last! She'd be able to bake cakes and try out some new recipes. Julian didn't seem to notice what she cooked from one week to the next since the accident.

'It sounds nice! I come from a small village myself, so I think I'll feel quite happy here.' Alex stood up. 'After that great meal, I'd better start earning my keep.'

2

Alex picked up some more hand-written pages from the desk. 'Why don't you use a dictaphone? It would be quicker than writing longhand, and leave you more time for other things. Oh, by the way, I found a complete translation of that Greek philosopher's work you were searching for on the Internet. I've noted the source for you.' She tore a page out of her notebook, and handed him the address. She wondered what Julian Cordell would look like when his serious grey eyes were alight with laughter; he was a serious man.

There was a hint of a frown and faint lines wrinkled his brow as he replied. 'Hmm! A dictaphone makes sense, of course, but I'd like to keep track of my alterations. I might want to refer back and compare. I need the various versions in black and white to do that.'

Alex adjusted the jonquil coloured silk scarf at her neck. 'That's the great thing about a computer; it can keep track of everything. I can store as many versions of your text as you like, and keep them in a numbered order — marking alterations in colour until you decide on the final one. You can have a print out of every chapter with the changes you make as we go along. In effect, it's like before, but without the pen-work.'

He gave her a brief smile and leaned back in his chair. Alex mused that although it was just a quick smile, it made him look so much younger.

He tilted his head to the side. 'It sounds like your computer is almost capable of writing this book on its own; I'm beginning to feel superfluous!'

Alex was unaware of the attractive picture she presented when she returned his smile. She played with the notebook in her hands and his eyes were drawn to her slender, pink-tipped fingers. 'There's no danger of that! A computer will never replace the human brain. A computer can do away with a lot of the boring mechanical processes, but it can't think independently, bring history to life like you do, or give the readers a chance to use their imagination.'

His eyebrows raised a fraction in silent inquiry. Alex grew silent, then hurried on to explain. 'I was curious to see what your other books were like. I read *The Etruscans* last weekend. I enjoyed it; it was informative and entertaining.'

There was more than a hint of pleasure in his voice when he replied. He twisted the pen resting in his hands, and met her eyes. 'Thank you! I'm glad you liked it.'

She broke the eye contact with him. Alex felt how her cheeks were too pink. 'What do you think about the dicta-phone? Want to give it a try?'

He nodded. 'I've used them before, although I prefer to write rather than to speak into a machine — still, we have to use time efficiently. Where can we get one?'

'I have one in my car. They are so small these days; don't take up any room,' she explained breathlessly. Glancing quickly at her watch, she was almost glad to get away from him for a couple of minutes, so that she could order her thoughts.

He nodded with an expression of good humour. 'Fine! Good, that leaves me time to fill your dictaphone with the end of the next chapter, and probably enough time to check some facts that come up in the next.' Reaching down to fondle Josh's silky head, he continued, 'I'll take Josh as far as the garden gate first, otherwise he's bound to start to fret when I don't want to be disturbed.'

Alex's eyes were drawn to his hand stroking the dog's head and the rough texture of his navy fisherman sweater. She shook herself and made a hasty exit. Just over a fortnight ago she'd wondered if she'd get on with this man, and now she found herself sometimes wishing she could supply him with some crumbs of comfort, and lighten his expression.

Julian continued to be cautious for a while, and confined their conversations to what was necessary and polite. He also kept a close eye on what she did. Julian recognised that she knew her job, was working hard, and he soon admitted she was taking more research work off his hands than he expected.

The atmosphere improved by leaps and bounds.

Julian and Annie had a companionable relationship. Annie could say things to him, and even nag him a little, and he took it in good part. He didn't necessarily react as Annie wanted him to, but he listened patiently and pretended to take heed. Julian often teased her; a facet of his character that gave Alex a glimpse of the man he was before fate dealt him some bad cards.

Julian and Annie had gone through the trauma of the accident and its aftermath together, and it had forged a strong bond between them. Luckily

Alex also got on with Annie from the word go. Annie was a down-to-earth, uncomplicated soul. She was clearly devoted to Julian, and she was generous and hospitable to others by nature. She enjoyed having Alex's company in the house after a couple of years of sole male presence.

Two-and-a-half weeks after her arrival, Alex was sitting with Annie in the kitchen feeling completely at home. Despite Annie's protests, Alex had helped her wash the dishes after the evening meal, and Annie felt she deserved an extra treat. Julian had gone, as usual, to listen to the evening news.

'Here Alex, try one of these!'

'Gosh, I'm going to end up like the back end of a bus if this goes on for a couple of months. The evening meal was wonderful, and now you're tempting me again.'

'Oh, go on with you! You know I love cooking. You're slim as a reed.'

Alex laughed, and sucked the tips of her fingers as she finished a light-as-air pastry, covered in melted jam and coconut. 'Umm! That was lovely, but it's all I'm allowing myself today. Enough is enough!'

Annie settled contentedly in her chair, straightened some soft folds in her pink pullover, and interlaced her arms across her chest. Alex already recognised the signs — Annie was ready for a chat. 'You've never explained why you came here. It's a quiet village. Wasn't there any work where you lived?'

Alex tensed for a moment, but knew that Annie had experienced enough of life's disappointment herself; she didn't find it hard to explain. Alex swallowed and found her voice. 'I wanted to get away; to cut short explanations — because of a man!'

Annie's lips pursed slightly, her eyes widened in interest, and she leaned slightly forward, waiting for Alex to continue.

Alex searched for the right words. 'Two years ago Tony and I decided to found a secretarial agency. We met through a mutual friend and the idea just grew when we were talking about how great it would be to be your own boss. In the beginning we shared the work as it came in. Tony is an accountant so he was able to cover areas I couldn't. It was an uphill fight to make ends meet for quite a time.'

Alex cradled the teacup and took a sip. 'Slowly we earned a good reputation, and as the firm got more and more customers, we were able to take on some part-timers. Tony continued to cover any accounting tasks that came in, and he also took over the job of finding and cultivating new clients. I handled the organisation of the company and worked as a secretary. If we had too much to do ourselves, we filled the gap with our temps. It would have worked out fine if our business relationship hadn't turned into a personal one too.'

Anger knotted her stomach as she remembered. 'I thought I'd fallen in love with him, and he with me; he played the part of my boyfriend to perfection. I never doubted his affection and I trusted him completely. We were even vaguely talking about getting engaged soon.' Annie leaned forward to fill Alex's cup again, and Alex continued. 'One day, I found out by chance that he'd been having an affair, with the wife of one of our best clients. You know how these things happen — a friend of a friend found out, that led to gossip, a lot of speculation, and eventually confrontation. Apparently, it had been going on for quite some time.' She gave Annie a resigned shrug and a weak smile.

Annie smiled back sympathetically and waited expectantly for Alex to go on. She wasn't disappointed; Alex did.

'I ended our partnership, private and personal, as soon as I found out, and decided the best thing would be to move away for a while. Friends tried to persuade me to stick around and not give him the chance to pretend nothing had happened, but I wanted to let grass grow over things. That's when I saw Julian's advert in the paper.'

Annie's voice was kind-hearted. 'The best thing you could have done. He sounds like someone who wants to keep his cake, and eat it. Forget him, my dear! You deserve someone better and you'll meet someone better, I'm sure.'

Alex wasn't surprised to see how Annie had boxed and classified Tony, even though she didn't know him. That was Annie to a T . . . Life had taught her it was easier to live by the rules. If you loved someone, you were faithful, and if you got cheated you acted accordingly.

Alex wasn't sad about Tony any more; she didn't even miss him. She wondered if she had ever really loved him; she reasoned that if she had, she ought to be heartbroken, but she wasn't. She was angry with him and terribly disappointed, but she saw him now for what he was, and could talk about him without regret.

Alex tossed her head, and her eyebrows arched mischievously. 'I'm definitely not looking for a new boyfriend at the moment, Annie. I can earn my own living, and I've got a supportive family and some good friends. If I'm lucky I will meet someone worth loving, but if I don't, I don't. Once bitten and twice shy, as the saying goes!'

The doorbell interrupted their conversation. Annie looked at the clock and got up. 'That'll be Doctor Arden! He often calls on Tuesdays. Julian won't make the effort to go to see him regularly, so he comes here. He's a friend of Julian's too. Back in a jiff; have another cake!'

Annie bustled out and Alex reflected that she was glad she'd found this job. Fate had been kind. How could she have misjudged Tony so badly? She circled the rim of her teacup with her finger, and drew a little comfort from the knowledge that in the end it had been easy to leave him. She remembered how he'd blustered when she'd confronted him with the truth, but still continued to lie blatantly. The legal split up of the company was still in progress. As long as she came out of it without any debts, she didn't care — the firm was a thing of the past.

A short time later, Alex heard voices approaching, and the door opened to reveal Annie following a stranger into the room. She also caught the end of their conversation.

The man's voice was pleasant and genial. 'If only he'd think about it; study the details and find out what's involved. Even if it does mean another operation and more physiotherapy, the chances of success are good. Can't you persuade him, Annie?'

Annie shook her head vigorously. 'He won't listen to anyone, not even his sister. Sophie tried to talk him into it, last time she was here.'

The man bent his head to come through the door. Alex guessed that he was in his late thirties with ash blond hair and blue eyes. He smiled easily in

Alex's direction; the skin around his eyes crinkled. He had a kindly philosophical expression.

Annie did the introductions. 'Alex, this is Dr Arden. I've brought him in to have a cup of tea before he goes again. Doctor, this is Alex Paxton.'

He held out his hand and Alex gripped it briefly. She said, 'Hello! I hope you're hungry. If you don't help me to eat Annie's cakes, I'm likely to turn up at your surgery an overweight wreck.'

He laughed. 'I'll help demolish some of these gladly! Annie makes such wonderful cakes. My visits to Julian are just cover-ups, I'm afraid.' He gestured towards the cake stand laden with small cakes in the middle of the table. 'Annie collects prizes at the bazaar every year, don't you Annie? And, not without reason.'

Annie smiled broadly. 'Oh, go on with you! Flattery will get you anywhere, Doctor! Sit down, I'll make some fresh tea.'

He sat down on one of the

farmhouse chairs and made himself comfortable. 'So, you're a new face in the village. How do you like it here, so far?' He pushed a strand of hair that had flopped on to his forehead.

'Very much. The weather is still unsettled, but as soon as I can, I intend to walk and see a bit of the surrounding countryside. Everyone is very friendly, and what surprises me most is that somehow they all know who I am, and what I'm doing here.'

Munching his way contentedly through a couple of the small cakes, he nodded. 'I bet! The telegraph system in the village is amazing. Sometimes I think that everyone knows what I'm going to do, before I do myself.' He smiled across at her.

Alex chuckled. 'That's the price for living in a small place; but it does have advantages too. Who would exchange this place for the anonymity of a city?'

He answered promptly. 'Young people, and yuppies! But I agree with you. Most people hereabouts are my patients, so I know them well. The majority of them are the salt of the earth.' He looked at his watch. 'I must get a move on. I've one more call before evening surgery.' He looked at Annie. 'Tom Simpson . . . he's got a bad bout of bronchitis. Since Nelly died, he doesn't take proper care of himself.'

'He's not the only one. You ought to find yourself a wife, Doctor, or you'll end up like Tom one day! I'm making beef stew tomorrow. I'll take him some for lunch.'

Keith glanced at the grin on Alex's face, and his mouth twitched in answer. 'I knew I could count on you, Annie.' He stood up. 'Well, goodnight, Miss Paxton.'

'That makes me feel ancient. Please call me Alex.'

'Pleasure! But only if you call me Keith.' She nodded.

He picked up his bag, and lifted his hand in a gesture of farewell. His footsteps echoed down the hallway as Annie accompanied him soft-footed in her sensible slippers.

3

Alex popped her head around the kitchen door — 'I'm going for a walk, Annie. The weather is lovely at the moment. Who knows how long it will last.'

Annie was sitting in the only armchair in the room, with her feet propped up on one of the dining chairs. The chair bulged in the wrong places, but it was clearly Annie's favourite haven. She nodded. 'Can't expect anything else at this time of year.' She looked over the rim of her glasses, eyeing Alex's yellow windproof anorak and jeans. 'When you're dressed properly, it doesn't matter. April weather is like that; it's unpredictable! Take Josh, he needs some exercise. That dog lies around too much.'

'Right, I'll ask Professor Cordell.'

'For goodness sake, girl! Call him Julian!'

Alex tendered her explanation. 'I can't call him that; he's my employer. It's usual to call employers by their surname. It keeps things professional.'

With a vague hint of disapproval in her voice, Annie retaliated — 'Huh! Professional, my hat! Don't be so daft girl — you're living in the same house, eating the same food, using the same rooms; that's not the same as working for someone you only see in an office for a couple of hours a day. Still it's none of my business. Don't be late back, Julian's sister rang earlier to say she's coming for tea.'

Alex's eyes were bright with merriment as she closed the door and made her way down the shadowed corridor to the study. Annie had a soft heart — although she could be a bit bossy sometimes. Alex knocked and lifted the latch.

'I'm going for a walk ... ' She stopped in mid-sentence when she saw a man sitting in an armchair opposite Julian. She didn't need to guess who he was; he was wearing a dog collar. 'Oh, sorry! I didn't mean to interrupt.'

Julian was dressed in a black polo shirt and black chinos. Alex noticed that he tended to wear dark colours all the time — usually navy blue, black or dark grey. His clothes were clearly expensive, casual in style, and they suited him; he always looked smart without looking too stiff and too immaculate. He looked up from the dark leather chair and said. 'Come in, Alex! Meet Tom Elton, our local vicar.'

Alex advanced into the room and took the outstretched hand of the slight, middle-aged man. 'Pleased to meet you, Vicar.'

'My pleasure, my dear.' I've already heard about Julian's assistant. His voice was low and apologetic. 'Although they shouldn't, people in the village do gossip. I try in vain to call a halt. Thankfully usually it's quite harmless.'

She smiled. 'That's quite normal in a village, I think.' Alex noticed the chessboard on the table between the two men. 'I won't disturb you. I'm going for a walk, and came to ask if I could take Josh.' At the sound of his name, the retriever's tail began to thump loudly on the planked floor. He leapt up and trotted across to join Alex. She automatically fondled his head.

Julian's eyebrows lifted in amusement. 'Just look at that, Tom! He deserts me without a backward glance.'

Alex flushed. 'Nonsense, you know he's devoted to you; he just wants to get out.' She waited. 'May I?'

Julian turned away, his expression hidden as he stared down at the chessboard. He looked up at her again, stretched his arms behind his head and the shirt stretched across his chest for a moment. He then picked up one of the figures he'd already won from his opponent. 'Of course, take him he needs all the exercise he can get. He's obedient, but keep him in sight, and put him on the lead if there are sheep about. The farmers get annoyed if they see a dog near their sheep.' He looked around. 'His lead must be . . . on the hallstand.'

Alex remained silent and just nodded. She wondered how often he thought about the fact that he couldn't do things that other people took for granted any more. Just taking the dog for a walk was a monumental effort if you had to do so with crutches under your arms. According to what she heard Dr Arden say, he had a chance to improve the situation. Why didn't he grab it with both hands? She wondered if there was a mental block.

She slapped the side of her jeans. 'Come on, Josh!' With Josh dancing at her feet she went towards the door, and closed it softly behind her.

Alex went through the garden with its level pathway and passed through the half-gate in the fence at the back. She let Josh off the lead as soon as they reached open ground. He pranced around in delight, racing ahead, following tantalising scents, with an eye on Alex's progress. Alex followed a path meandering along crumbling stonewalls that were intercepted here and there by patches of thorn hedging towards the distant foothills.

Wandering groups of black and white bleating sheep eyed Josh nervously from a safe distance; Alex put him on the lead. She was sure he was no danger to them, but she stuck to Julian's instructions.

The scenery was wild and beautiful. In the distance the road dipped and rose again before it finally vanished over the long drift of the fells. There was a cold freshness in the gentle wind that lifted her hair.

She'd discovered from the odd conversation about the district with Julian, that some famous people, including Wordsworth, and Bronwell Bronte, had spent part of their lives nearby; and she was beginning to understand why the valley had been a source of inspiration and pleasure to them. She left the rough track for a gentler one climbing to the crest of a rise, and then suddenly all the fells were open before her.

On all sides the land seemed to be cradled in timeless suspension. She picked up some sticks, sat down on a crumbling wall that ambled downwards out of sight. With her back to the wind, she began unconsciously kicking her heels against the rough stones — a bad habit she'd got into as a child. There were no sheep in sight, so she let Josh off the lead and threw the sticks for him to retrieve.

Alex viewed the panorama and let her thoughts wander. The sun was welcomingly warm on her face, even though dark clouds were gathering on the horizon. She wondered why Julian stubbornly refused to try any new treatment. 'He's an obstinate man. Damaged inside as well as out.' She brushed her hair out of her face and spoke out loud, before she threw another stick in a wide arc. 'He's punishing himself, for no reason at all.' Picking up another stick from the bundle at her side, she was shocked to hear a voice drifting over her shoulder.

'Talking to yourself, Alex?'

Taken by surprise, her hand flew automatically to her mouth. She was relieved to see it was Keith Arden, and not a stranger. He smiled at her, and she relaxed again. 'Oh, heavens! You gave me a fright. Where did you come from?'

'I've been out walking over in that direction.' He indicated with his chin. 'I'm on my way back now.' He stared pointedly at the horizon where wild and angry looking grey clouds were gathering and moving across the sky in unseemly haste. 'If you'll take my advice, you won't go any further either. There's a storm threatening.'

She jumped down and brushed her jeans. 'Yes, it looks pretty menacing, doesn't it? If you don't mind I'll walk back with you, I was thinking of going home anyway. Josh!' Alex put him on the lead again and the dog trotted ahead of them, as far as the leash allowed.

He broke the silence. 'I couldn't help catching what you said. Were you muttering to yourself about Julian back there, by any chance?'

She flushed. 'Yes. I gather that you think some new treatment might help him. I was just wondering why he won't give it a try. Surely he should be over the moon to know there might be hope for improvement, or even complete recovery?' Alex felt easy in Keith Arden's company; and she had no inhibitions about what she said.

'You'll understand why I shouldn't comment too much, but as his friend, I have to admit his situation is more complicated than it may seem to an outsider. Apart from the physical damage he got, he also had to cope with the loss of his wife. It was a terribly hard time for him, to put it mildly. He's still labouring under the after-effects.'

'Did you know her? His wife?'

'Gillian? Yes, but not very well. I'd only been in the village about a year before the accident happened. Julian and Gillian had settle here a couple of years previous to that. I know that Gillian was the only child of some well-known, wealthy industrialist and unfortunately he died not long after his daughter — perhaps the shock was too much for him. He left everything to Julian, so he doesn't have any serious financial pressures any more. He can afford to step back from teaching and concentrate on writing. Julian was already well-known as a writer before the accident happened anyway.'

She couldn't help herself. 'What was she like?'

'Gillian?' He paused, and turned towards her, looking at her speculatively for a moment. 'She was very attractive, a determined young woman, with lots of energy and charm, and from what I gather she usually got what she wanted. She was a cosseted daughter before her marriage, so her lifestyle didn't change much afterwards. I don't think she had a job. Anyway I don't remember that she had one.'

She nodded. 'Thanks! I didn't want to ask Julian, or even Annie come to that, but I was curious. Julian might bite my head off, and Annie will probably have conflicting loyalties; she's fiercely devoted to Julian.'

He shoved his hand in his pocket. 'Yes, Julian is lucky to have someone like Annie around. She is worth her weight in gold.'

Alex tried to explain away her interest. 'I just wondered what kind of person Gillian was. I think it would help me to understand the situation better, and make things easier for me to fit in. If she'd survived the accident things would have turned out differently for them all.'

'Ah, yes. But that's a big 'if'. Life never turns out as you expect it to. Gillian was killed, and Julian survived. Did you know he was driving the car?'

Alex nodded, and he continued. 'The inquest came to the conclusion he wasn't responsible. He hit a patch of black ice and slid uncontrollably into the path of an oncoming vehicle on the other side of the road. He paid a terrible price for what happened — Gillian's death. Trouble is, he still hasn't found a way to put it behind him, and he still seems to go on punishing himself.' Keith shifted his weight, and eyed her prudently.

Alex decided she'd questioned him enough. She moved on to other topics, and asked him where he came from. By the time they reached the garden gate, Alex had corroborated her original opinion about him — he was a thoroughly nice person.

Keith had intended to leave her at the garden gate, to go down the lane past the church to his cottage, but Annie spotted him from the kitchen window. She came to the door to wave a teacloth and shouted.

'Join us, Doctor. You're just in time for tea.' Annie eyed Josh's dirty legs. 'Wipe him down, Alex!' She reached to the side of the door to hand Alex an old towel kept there for that purpose. She motioned them both into the kitchen. 'Take off your coat, Doctor! Come through to the sitting room for some tea if you have time. Sophie's here.'

'Sophie?' Alex asked, while rubbing Josh's fur, and noticing her shoes were almost as dirty as the dog's paws.

Keith provided the necessary information. 'Julian's sister. Thanks, Annie! I will.'

Alex stood up and hung the towel on the hook. 'Oh right, but I'll just change my shoes first!' Alex left her shoes outside the kitchen door, glanced at her tangled hair in the hall mirror in passing, and ran up the stairs two at a time.

Alex changed her shoes quickly and ran a comb through her hair. She automatically pulled the pale lilac sweater tidily into place again over the navy trousers, added a little more lipstick, and checked her reflection in the mirror before hurrying down the stairs again. She came to an abrupt halt halfway, as she heard raised voices coming from the study. Since her arrival, she'd never heard Julian so loud; he also sounded very angry. The other voice was a woman's.

'Sophie! It's my decision and mine alone, so leave it!'

'You're as stubborn as a mule.' There was a scraping of a chair across the parquet floor and the door opened. Alex had a back view of a slight female figure hurrying down the hallway.

She'd left the door to the study slightly ajar, and some instinct drove Alex to tap it quietly and go in. He was behind his desk; his face was stern and his eyes were stormy sheets of grey ice. Alex was lost for words for a second and wondered if she had the right to interfere. Although she dared not admit it to anyone, least of all herself, she had grown to care about Julian and how he coped with his life.

Alex crossed her fingers and hoped he accepted her enough now to listen to her comments. 'I couldn't help hearing; I was coming down the stairs. I hope you don't mind me butting in? Can I help at all?'

She sat down uninvited in the chair opposite him and laced her fingers in her lap. His expression was grim and there was a prolonged silence. It was oppressive, and she felt uncomfortable; she almost believed she'd made a mistake and should have left him alone after all. She was about to hoist herself to her feet again, when he gestured vaguely with his hand for her to stay where she was. She guessed that he was trying hard to give her the impression of normality, although his voice was still coloured with mockery when he finally spoke.

'Do you happen to have any brothers or sisters?'

'One brother.'

His grey eyes looked even darker than usual as he held her gaze. 'Do you get on with him?'

'On the whole? Yes! Although we used to bicker a lot when we were small. He thought he was entitled to boss me around.' She smiled at him, hoping to soothe the atmosphere a little. She was rewarded with an understanding look. 'Disagreement between siblings is quite normal, isn't it?'

He started to talk to her as if he hadn't been listening to what she said, although Alex knew from experience that he had. 'Yes, but normally you do grow out of arguing with each other, don't you? My sister hasn't reached that stage of development yet. She assumes she has an answer to every problem under the sun, especially my problems.'

Alex cleared her throat. 'I'm sure she only wants what is best for you. She cares; otherwise she wouldn't bother, would she? Affection reveals itself in many different ways.'

His expression lightened a fraction; he gazed at her speculatively, and then finally gave a hollow sounding laugh. 'You're right, I know she's trying to be kind, but it doesn't make things easy. The days of squabbling for dominance in the nursery are past, but Sophie doesn't seem to comprehend that. My sister thinks she's in charge.'

She took a deep breath and hoped he wouldn't get annoyed with her. 'It's none of my business, and I hope you won't think that I'm trying to interfere, but has this something to do with whether or not you should try some new treatment?' She added quickly as an explanation. 'You must realise that it isn't easy to live in this house and not pick up all kinds of information that is none of my business and has nothing to do with me.'

He moved his shoulders in a shrug of anger, and his brows drew together in a dark frown. 'Of course! What else? Keith thinks there's a chance — another operation. That is enough to send Sophie into action, like a whirling dervish.'

She licked her lips and spoke with deceptive calm. 'Even when you feel she seems to be pushing you, you ought to give her the benefit of the doubt. It's only because she cares and wants to help.'

He answered sharply and clenched his mouth tighter. 'I'm not going through hell again unless someone can give me a guarantee. Even Keith can't do that; every operation constitutes a degree of risk. I don't want to end up worse off than I am now. No-one seems to think about that. My life may be far from perfect, but I'm managing to do the things that give me pleasure and are important to me. I can do without vague promises of a better future unless someone assures me of success.'

A sense of inadequacy swept over her, and sympathy too. 'If that's what you feel, why not just explain it to her? You're used to formulating words, it should be peanuts for you to present your point of view. She cares about your well-being; make her accept your decision by telling her what you want, and why.'

He stared across at her with empty eyes; the skin was tight on his cheeks. 'Quite a little philosopher aren't you . . . old beyond your years . . . '

Pausing, he gazed at her speculatively and ran his hand over his face. The expression softened. 'Sorry, Alex! I've no reason to be crotchety with you as well — I didn't mean to be caustic.' He sighed heavily. 'You're right. Usually I can cope. She caught me on the wrong footing today, my hip is hurting like mad. Join the others! I'll be along in a minute.'

It was the first time Alex had ever heard him admit he was in pain. She rose, and wished she could wave a magic wand and release him from a life that seemed one long bitter battle. She nodded silently and left the room, closing the door as she went.

4

His sister bore no great resemblance to him; their colouring was different and Alex guessed she was a couple of years younger. She had an interesting oval face, light brown hair, lively brown eyes and a clear complexion. Annie introduced the two women to each other, and waved Alex in the direction of an empty chair. Keith smiled across at Alex as she accepted some sandwiches and a piece of cake from Annie.

Annie was talking to Sophie. 'Oh, he's just stubborn. You know that it's impossible to move him once he's made up his mind.'

Sophie Cordell nodded at the housekeeper and hooked the handle of the teacup that was in front of her. Her voice was soft and musical. 'Yes, but usually I can get him to see reason. Why won't he listen this time?'

Alex couldn't stop herself. 'Isn't it better just to leave him alone to make his own decision? It's his life. I'm sure he thinks seriously about all the pros and cons if he's got all the information. Perhaps he will come round to your way of thinking, perhaps not — but I'm sure heckling won't help.'

Sophie looked up and across at Alex in surprise. Her mouth was slightly open and Alex waited for a possible rebuke, because it was all none of her business, and she was only Julian's employee.

Instead, to Alex's relief, Sophie let out a gentle laugh.

'You're perfectly right. It's completely useless to tell Julian what he should, or should not do. He's always been the same. And I certainly don't want to drive a wedge between us by tormenting him all the time; on the whole we've always got on very well. You know Julian well, considering you've only known him a short time. You're Alex?'

Alex nodded.

'May I call you Alex?'

'Of course! I hope you don't think I was being rude?'

Further conversation was interrupted temporarily when Julian opened the door, and joined them at the table. They were all silent for a moment. He paused at his sister's chair and ruffled her hair before he sat down next to her. Sophie grinned back at him wordlessly, but touched his cheek briefly, before she looked at Alex again and winked.

'How do you cope with working for this monster, Alex?'

'Oh . . . it's easy once you've mastered the art. Your brother is just an average one. There are worse examples, believe me.' She glanced at Julian.

An eyebrow was arched and the beginning of a smile tipped the corners of Julian's mouth. 'I've been called all kinds of things in my life, but the term 'monster' is new, and a whacking exaggeration!'

With a giddy sense of pleasure, she realised they'd crossed a dividing line and that he'd lowered his safeguard long enough for her to know that he accepted her on his own terms. He hadn't ranted or raved at her comments about Sophie and him, he'd listened and absorbed what she said.

The rest of tea went well. The others at the table talked about things and happenings that meant nothing to Alex, but she didn't mind. She joined in whenever suitable, but on the whole was content to lean back and be a silent observer. Julian and his sister were clearly back on good terms again. Alex saw that Keith Arden viewed Julian's sister with an expression in his eyes that signalled more than an average interest. Alex wondered if Sophie realised it.

Julian for his part sometimes let his glance slide back and forth between Alex and Keith. They got on well, although that didn't surprise him. Keith was a good friend and a decent chap, and Alex was a sensible and appealing girl. He just wondered if they'd get attracted to each other, and how Sophie would react if they did. He guessed that it might upset Sophie. She'd never said so, but Julian knew that Sophie admired Keith a lot, and he also had a secret wish that their friendship would end in love one day — for Sophie's sake.

At an appropriate moment Alex asked, 'What do you do for a living, Sophie?'

'Librarian.'

'Like your job?'

'On the whole, yes. Although I do get the odd day when I'd like to storm out of the place. It doesn't happen very often though. I always wanted to work with books, so it was either a bookshop, or the library for me.'

Julian cut in. 'She used to arrange our books in alphabetical order, and even put them into categories, as soon as she could read properly. She's always had this need for systematic order — in contrast to me. I have my own methods, Alex, as you know.'

Alex rewarded him with a wry expression. 'I can't pretend that I make head or tail of it. Your shelves are a disaster area as far as I'm concerned.'

Sophie butted in with, 'I'd love to get my hands on your study. It's a shambles.'

Julian gave a short and pointed laugh. 'Not a chance! It may be a 'disaster area' or a 'shambles' to other people, but it is organised. I know where things are, no matter what it looks like.'

By the end of the afternoon, Alex found she'd spent an enjoyable time. Sophie was unpretentious, and she already liked Keith. The tea party broke up when Sophie said that she had to go back to town, as she was meeting friends that evening. Alex thought that she saw a glint of disappointment in Keith's eyes.

Julian went with Sophie and Keith to see them off. From the bathroom she saw Sophie and Keith standing by Sophie's car. They spoke for a while and then shook hands. He held her hand longer than necessary, and Alex smiled as she turned away.

The weeks passed and the work

progressed. Lots of half-finished text marked with coloured tags collected in piles all over Julian's study. Most of the day she worked on her own, upstairs in a small bedroom that had been temporarily turned into an office. The final submission date hung over them. Alex could see that Julian was extremely efficient and professional about his work.

On one of the rare moments when she could sit back and observe him she thought that despite the fact that he couldn't walk, he still had a powerful, muscled chest and that he'd learned to compensate for his lack of walking mobility with economic movements elsewhere.

Now that Alex was used to seeing him all the time, and they were on a more relaxed basis she wondered why she was still nervous with him and admitted that he disturbed her equilibrium.

Sometimes she felt such a strong surge of affection for him, it worried her. She'd never experienced the same kind of feeling for any of her previous employers before and she put it down to pure sympathy for the way he coped with his physical impediment.

Now and then he received a small amount of fan mail, and that was always welcomed as a short respite from the daily slog. There were often requests for him to give talks, attend seminars or conferences; he invariably dictated a polite refusal. Just this morning a letter had arrived from a former colleague at university, asking if Julian would be interested in a part-time professorship in the history department as they were about to advertise for someone. Julian skimmed the text and put the letter aside quickly again before he began to shuffle other papers impatiently.

'Would you like to dictate a reply?'

His voice was colourless. 'No, just send the usual thing. Thanks, regrets, other commitments, etc. etc.' He buried his attention in a book on the desk.

'You used to teach at a university?'

He didn't look up. 'Yes, for a couple of years.'

'Did you dislike the work?'

He faltered for a moment as he thought back over the years. 'No, I enjoyed it very much. It was a good time and a great equaliser to theoretical academics.'

Her response was automatic. 'I bet you were a good lecturer.'

A wry but indulgent glint appeared in his dark-grey eyes as he glanced up at her again. 'Do you? Why is that?'

'Because you have a gift of bringing the past to life, and you probably made your students aware of the less noticeable threads that led up to certain developments and made them more enthusiastic about history.'

A flash of real humour crossed his face. 'You give me too much credit!'

'If you used to enjoy it, why don't you do it again?' She looked at the address. 'The university isn't so far. Wouldn't . . .'

He shook his head decisively, the

humour faded, and his jaw clenched. 'Crutches are not suitable to point students the way from the past to the present.'

Alex thought briefly about giving in to an impulse to scream at him. She didn't scream, but she threw caution to the wind. 'You realise that you are pretty feather-brained about some things, don't you? Youngsters are not stupid; and university students are interested in your ability, not disability. Of course they'd sympathise with you, but sympathy is not pity. They'd see the person and not the crutches. You are the only one who pities yourself . . . and in my opinion, you do it much too often.'

She grabbed the pile of corrections waiting for her on the desk, and stormed out of the room with blazing cheeks. She left him with his lips parted in surprise. After a minute, the self-same lips curved themselves into an unconscious smile again.

Neither of them referred to her remarks later, he signed the refusal without any more comment. He did at least add a personal line or two to the foot of the page.

Julian insisted she kept to office hours and finished punctually every day. There was no panic yet to finish the book, so she didn't protest. She could increase her input later, if it was necessary. Alex knew he was busy long after she left, and that he often continued checking references and doing research work even after the evening meal. Alex was happy to turn her attention to more mundane things.

The weather grew milder, and daylight lingered longer. She took Josh out regularly for long walks and relished the long rambles almost as much as the dog. Sometimes she met Keith going for a ramble, or on her way home.

One afternoon Julian was making a sandwich and watched them standing at the garden gate chatting. Keith had also mentioned her name sometimes in the conversation when he called, and it gave Julian an empty feeling just to listen to someone else talking about her. It was surprising how quickly she had become a part of this house and his life.

Alex went home to visit her parents and friends, but she admitted to herself that by now she was just as happy to stay in Charter House with Annie and Julian. If she stayed, she enjoyed the special quiet of the weekend and often used the time to catch up on reading or television. She went shopping with Annie to Coniston a couple of times.

Despite the fact that Alex protested that it wouldn't be worth her joining, the owner of the teashop persuaded her to help out with the local dramatic society. They didn't expect her to act — they all knew she wouldn't be here when the play was to be presented — but they needed help with the scenery and the costumes, and they also roped her in to find props, something which often brought her in contact with people she'd never met till then. She followed the instruction to 'try Sadie', or 'ask Bert, he has one' and the circle of people she got to know in the village grew. She also was given the task of making tea. After rehearsals they all went to the local pub for a parting drink.

One Thursday afternoon after work, coming back from a walk with Josh and humming gently to herself, she found Julian sitting in the arbour in the garden. Josh spotted him there long before she did, and dashed towards him in a frenzy of excitement. Alex followed at a more sedate pace. She folded the dog's lead in her hands and sat down on the stone bench next to him. He stroked the dog's head with his long fingers. He looked at her and disarmed her with one of his rare smiles. Her pulse increased noticeably.

'You're stealing my dog's heart, Alex.' He liked the way she always managed to look neat, and noted that she had a way with colour. The pale green pullover and patterned paisley scarf were a perfect foil for her hair and eyes.

'Josh has mine, so it's a fair exchange. I'll miss him when I go.' She looked around at everything and nothing in particular. She avoided his face. Office business was neutral and it was easier to keep him in the right perspective. He was her boss there, moments like this and here in the garden where they were alone and physically so close, he was just a man, and the two situations were completely different.

Alex told herself not to imagine things. Just because his stand-offishness had melted away there was no reason to put too much meaning into it.

'Isn't it lovely this afternoon? It's great to have good weather at last? The flowers are waiting to burst into bloom. I've followed their progress ever since I arrived and this garden will be a huge splash of colour soon.'

He nodded. 'All thanks to Bill Watson; he does a marvellous job considering that he only comes for a couple of hours once a week. I could let it run wild I suppose, but Gill loved the garden so I decided to keep it going.'

Alex swallowed hard, it was the first time she'd ever heard him speak voluntarily about his wife. 'Did she . . . did she plan the garden on her own?'

He gave a shallow laugh and shook his head. 'Plan it? I suppose you could put it like that, yes! Work on it, no! Not much anyway. The garden was a wilderness when we moved in, and it took a lot of time and effort. She got ideas from all kinds of gardening books, some of which were totally unsuited to this area, and Bill did the physical part of trying to turn her ideas into reality. Bill warned her some things weren't worth trying. She was determined, but inevitably found out the hard way he was right. I sometimes wondered why he stayed; it certainly wasn't for the money. Lots of people want his help. Look at that rockery in the corner; a couple more days like this and it will be a rainbow of colours.'

She turned to look in the right direction. 'Did you . . . do you like gardening?'

'Not more than the average person. I used to potter about a bit until the accident, but if I get down on my knees now, I'd need a crane to get me up again.' He gave a hollow laugh. 'Still I'm not complaining. Bill manages without any help from me. I appreciate all his work but no, I'm not much of a gardener. What about you?'

She shook her head, and shrugged. The wind played gently with some strands of her hair and blew them across her face. She brushed them aside. 'Although I don't really know. My father is an enthusiastic gardener, he even grows vegetables; I like helping him now and then, but I suppose, you never know until you have your own garden whether you like gardening or not, do you?'

He appraised her lazily. 'It sounds like you get on with them? Your parents?'

'Umm! They're great; they're very supportive. They let me go my own way.'

He lifted one leg slowly over the other. 'My parents gave us freedom, but were strict about behaviour and respecting them and other people.'

She sighed contentedly. 'I'm going home this weekend.'

'Are you?' He looked over her head into the distance. 'The house will be quiet.'

'You make it sound like I cause mayhem when I'm here!'

He gave her a smile that sent her pulses racing, and shook his head. 'No I didn't mean that, only that you've livened the place up a bit since you arrived. I was hiding between, and behind the covers of books. Annie did her best to shake me out of it, but I didn't feel I was missing anything. I notice Annie is a lot more cheerful since you've arrived too. She loves having someone who praises her cooking.'

'That's easy.' She wrenched her

attention from his face and got up. She looked at her watch and used a female route of escape. 'I want to wash my hair before supper.'

She held out the lead. He took it, and nodded mechanically.

Alex turned away. For some reason she was glad to put distance between them. She was getting too involved, making too many silly speculations about how he functioned, what he was thinking. The weekend at home would clear her brain. She'd had a narrow escape with Tony, and was still susceptible. It was extremely stupid of her to imagine that Julian Cordell saw anything more in her than a secretarial assistant. He was just another employer.

5

Alex rang Sue as soon as she got in, and they arranged to go shopping together next day. After a morning of ransacking the shops, they finally made their way to their favourite bistro. Settled in one of the corner booths, they gave their order and leaned back.

Sue brushed the hair from her forehead with her hand. 'So, tell me about Julian Cordell, Alex. He sounds interesting.'

Alex suddenly realised that she must have mentioned Julian often during their telephone conversations; otherwise Sue wouldn't have stored it away in her memory. Alex hoped her tone of voice was non-committal.

'Julian? He's very good-looking; very intelligent, he's reserved and likeable . . . once you get to know him better.' Her eyes rested on the black and white marble tabletop as she spoke. The waitress arrived and it gave her a few more moments to gather her thoughts before she continued.

Sue stirred the frothy surface of her coffee and licked the spoon before she put it back on the saucer. 'To be honest, he sounds like good boyfriend material.'

Alex's cheeks turned a deep pink; she ran her fingers through her hair, and gave a hollow laugh. 'You're way off course there! He's mature and extremely clever. He's completely wrapped up in his work, and even if he wasn't married to the memory of his wife, he's the kind of man you couldn't just wheedle or hoodwink into an affair of some kind.'

Sue was watching her closely, so Alex paused for a moment and laughed weakly. 'If anyone wanted to get close, they'd have to face the prospect of removing the ghost of his wife from his memory. That would probably be a very difficult job, and it wouldn't be a very tempting one either.'

Sue caught the expression in her

friend's face and she heard the trace of exasperation in her voice. So, that's the way the wind was blowing, was it? She took a sip from the milky cappuccino. 'It must have been hard for him if the marriage was a good one, but the memories will eventually fade, and he'll move on. By the way, how do you feel about Tony? Do you still miss him; wish you were back together?'

Vehemently Alex shook her head. 'Looking back now, it was a blessing in disguise that I found out when I did. I realise that our attraction was based on being together too much, too often. Somehow I began to sense he needed idolisation, and he sensed I was looking for someone to love. As long as things went his way, Tony was a charmer — and he knew exactly how to use his charm.'

'I'm glad you split up! Most of our crowd never liked him. They accepted him because he was your boyfriend, not for his own sake. I was mad at the way he took advantage of you.'

'He made me feel special, Sue. I saw him through rose-coloured glasses. I didn't think he would ever cheat on me, I thought I was the centre of his life; that we were working towards the same future aims. I made an awful mistake and paid for it.'

'If it's a consolation, I think he realises that too now. He's having a hard time of it. I heard that the woman's husband intended to sue for divorce when he found out. She saw her comfortable lifestyle slipping away, so she dropped Tony like a hot potato, and she crawled back to her hubby. Everyone who knew you, and knew what had happened, more or less ignore him nowadays — and on top of that the agency is going downhill fast. A lot of the customers have already left for other agencies.'

Alex tossed her hair and gave her friend another weak smile. 'I'm sorry about that, but only because we both put a lot of work into creating the agency. I couldn't have gone on working with him; pretending nothing had happened. Perhaps some people would have — for the sake of the money, but money isn't everything.'

Sue nodded her head, agreeing energetically. 'It's his loss. You've picked yourself up and moved on, and I'm glad to see that you're more cheerful now than when you left. This new job has helped you recover. It is a shame about the agency, though, because you did the donkey-work, and made it successful, not Tony.'

Alex laughed softly at her friend's heated estimation. 'Don't forget he's a qualified accountant, and he was very good at his job, Sue. I don't think it's true that I did more for the agency than he did. Finding customers is a hard task too, but I won't argue with you because I just don't care. I'm over him and feel confident again. My present job with Julian has shown me there are worse things that can happen to people.'

'Will you come home again? When this job ends?'

Alex paused for a moment and considered the possibility. 'I don't know. Perhaps I'll go somewhere else; wherever fate takes me. I've made a break so if I get a job somewhere else why not?' She halted briefly. 'Hey! That's enough about me, what about your news? I know you and Stan are still going out together but are wedding bells on the horizon?'

Sue blushed faintly and admitted that Alex's assumption was right. Alex liked Stan, he was a cheery, steady chap, and Sue was her lifelong friend. Alex felt really happy for them. She listened to her friend's chatter as she filled in what had happened in the intervening weeks. Alex leaned back and relaxed. It hadn't been difficult to come back after all.

If Tony happened to walk into this bistro this minute, she'd be able to look at him without a pang or a regret. What she believed was love, had been only an illusion after all. She sighed contentedly, and was glad. She felt an invisible weight lift from her shoulders. She smiled encouragingly at Sue.

Julian spent the weekend doing research work and checking the latest version of the manuscript as far as they'd completed it. Annie went shopping to Coniston on Saturday, and the house was silent and peaceful. At first he enjoyed the quiet, but after a while he felt something was missing. It irritated him because he couldn't put his finger on exactly what. He found himself looking out of the window all the time, when he should be concentrating on the manuscript. He started momentarily when the shrill sound of the telephone broke the silence. He lifted the receiver. 'Hello!'

'Hello! My name's Tony Taylor. I'd like to speak to Alex please.'

Julian paused. 'Alex isn't here, I'm afraid.'

'Oh!' The voice was disappointed. 'When can I talk to her?'

'Not till Monday. She's gone home this weekend.'

The voice sounded bouncy and more

hopeful again. 'Really? I might bump into her then. Thanks! Sorry to have bothered you.'

'No problem! Do you want to leave a message?'

The man couldn't wait for the end of Julian's words. There was a click and the connection was broken. Julian turned back to his work, but he soon gave up any pretence of concentration. He pushed the papers to one side, and decided to go out with Josh. He went into the garden. He leaned on the gate for a support and threw sticks for Josh to retrieve. He tried not to think about the call, and tried not to wonder whom Tony Taylor was.

Annie returned in plenty of time to prepare the evening meal although Julian had told her to make a day of it, and he'd manage quite well on his own. Julian eyed her familiar warmth as she plonked her purchases on the kitchen table.

He said, 'I'm just about to make myself a pot of tea, want some?'

She smiled gratefully. 'That sounds just the thing. I'm parched!'

He filled the kettle, and Annie got the cups and saucers. She didn't hold with the modern-day habit of drinking everything out of mugs.

'So, what was your day like, Annie? Enjoy the bustle of the town?'

'Yes, it does me good sometimes. Not that I'm not glad to come home mind.'

Julian eyed the plastic bags. 'Bought anything special?'

Annie lifted down an old-fashioned biscuit barrel from the dresser, and took off the lid. 'Among other things, a lovely pair of shoes! It took me ages to find them.'

Julian munched at a biscuit and smiled. 'What colour this time?'

'A lovely shade of navy. I'll show you them in a minute.'

Julian shook his head in disbelief. 'I don't understand it. You must have dozens of pairs of shoes by now. What do you want them all for?'

'Men just don't understand. You

don't need a reason to buy a pair of shoes! Women can never have enough shoes and I can't resist, I never could.' She made herself comfortable and took a sip from the cup. 'What have you been doing? I hope you haven't sat at your desk all day and forgotten to get some fresh air.'

'Josh reminds me if I do, don't worry.' He twisted the spoon around in his hand absentmindedly. 'Oh, before I forget, someone called Tony Taylor phoned for Alex.'

'Huh! Did he?'

'What does, huh, mean! Does the name mean something to you?'

Annie gave a slight shrug of her shoulders. 'Only what Alex told me. I don't want to know him, thank you very much.'

His curiosity was wakened. 'Why?' He didn't usually listen too closely to Annie's gossiping, but this time he couldn't resist.

'I don't know if I should tell you. She told me about him once.'

He nodded and pretended not to be too interested. 'It's none of our business, but on the other hand, curiosity killed the cat.' He leaned forward.

Annie watched him thoughtfully. 'I don't suppose it does any harm to tell you. He cheated on her. They were almost engaged, and he was carrying on with someone else behind her back. She broke with him as soon as she found out.'

Julian was surprised how much the knowledge bothered him. He put on a nonchalant face and said, 'Oh, I see. Will you tell her that he rang?'

'Did he say he'd phone again?' Annie stirred her cup vigorously and the spoon rattled loudly as she put it back on the saucer.

He looked at her speculatively; he saw that Annie had taken sides, and nothing would budge her once she had. 'Just because you like Alex, doesn't mean you can interfere, Annie. You can't stop him phoning her. Perhaps they'll patch it up.'

Annie huffed audibly, and reached for the fruit bowl in the centre of the table. She started rearranging the apples. 'I wouldn't interfere, unless she wanted me to, but I don't think they'll patch it up. She's disillusioned, and I know her well enough to know she won't change her mind after the way he treated her.'

Julian nodded absentmindedly and felt relieved. He was tempted to discuss the situation further and get some more details, but he resisted.

6

Alex wasn't sorry to return to Charter House; she barely had time to take off her coat before Annie announced that she'd made Alex's favourite cake for afternoon tea, and Alex also found a bunch of cheerful yellow tulips on her bedside table.

Julian leaned back and linked his arms behind his head when she came into the office. 'The wanderer returns at last.' He was clearly in a very good mood, and his expression was friendly and relaxed — a very different person to the reserved employer she'd encountered on her arrival. Alex reflected that she'd grown to like the house, and its inhabitants very much; she was glad to be back.

After lunch, over a final cup of coffee, Annie brought her up to date with how she'd spent the weekend and listened to

Alex's news. Annie also told her that Tony had phoned. Annie was glad to see the news didn't impress Alex at all.

'He rang here; I wonder where he got the number from? He hasn't phoned my parents . . . Mum would have told me.' Alex shrugged. 'He's too scared to bother them.'

Annie forgot all her intentions about not interfering. 'I think I'd have been tempted to give him a piece of my mind. Julian spoke to him.'

Alex laughed softly. 'Tony doesn't take criticism very well. He'd lose his temper and tell you to mind your own business. He'd probably tell you relationships are very casual these days and that hardly anyone makes it to their golden wedding anniversary any more.' Alex guessed Annie had told Julian who Tony was. She felt uncomfortable at the thought they'd been talking about her.

'Humph! More the pity!'

Alex was amused by Annie's reaction. 'It's kind of you to worry . . . but if he phones again, I'll deal with him. It's not a problem any more, Annie.'

Julian didn't mention the phone call at all, and Alex was glad.

By the end of that week, the first five chapters were more or less completed. References had been checked, and the text had been polished to Julian's satisfaction. The selected pictures had to be fitted in, but the publishers were responsible for that. They were making real progress, and Julian seemed more cheerful than she'd ever seen him, even though they still had most of the work ahead of them.

Alex spent Friday tidying up all the loose ends and clearing her office of unwanted clutter. The prospect of a fairly quiet weekend was nipped in the bud when Julian's brother and his wife announced they were coming for a visit, and that Sophie was joining them on Sunday too. Although Julian muttered quietly to himself, and everyone else in general, about weekend researches being disrupted, Alex could see he was looking forward to seeing them. The news set Annie off in an immediate flurry.

Alex wished that she'd arranged to go home this weekend now, and wondered how she could keep out of sight and remain inconspicuous during the visit.

On Saturday morning Annie rushed through breakfast; she was intent on making finishing touches to the guest room. Alex and Julian faced each other across the breakfast table; a fresh breeze moved the green and white checked curtains, and Alex felt cold. She got up and closed the window. Julian looked up briefly, before he continued reading the morning paper. Without glancing at her, his voice startled her.

'You'll join us this evening, of course? Or have you got some other plan?'

She sat back momentarily lost for words. 'Join you?'

'Yes, for dinner with my brother and his wife.'

'Wouldn't you prefer to have just a family get-together? I don't mind watching TV in my room. You're not obliged to include me just because I live under your roof. Honestly!'

There was a teasing laughter as the dark grey eyes drew level with her hazel ones. 'I know that, Alex. It sounds like you think I'd expect you to scuttle away when visitors come; like Jane Eyre.' His mouth curved into a soft smile. 'It's just a family meal, nothing special. As you live here, you're very welcome.'

Alex was startled as a feeling of unexpected warmth surged through her as she looked at his expression.

He went on. 'I'm sure that my brother and his wife would like to meet you.'

After a moment of reflection under his waiting scrutiny, she agreed. Why not? 'I'll be glad to come.'

'Tell me something about them, Annie, so that I know what to expect. Alex leaned against the doorframe, her curved hips in soft navy trousers and her arms folded across a pale blue pullover. She watched as Annie polished the taps to a brilliant shine. The black and white bathroom was always spick and span, now it was fit for royalty.'

'Well . . . William doesn't look like Julian although he is also a very nice quiet character. Nicola sometimes appears to be a bit of a scatterbrain — well that's what people think. Personally I think she's a lot cleverer than anyone suspects. Just because she's blonde and bouncy doesn't mean that she's a featherbrain. They've been married about six years, and seem very happy.'

'What does William do? Do they have children? Does Nicola work?'

Annie folded a pile of soft white towels and put them on a glass shelf in the niche next to the bath. 'William is chief administrator of some big Trust, and Nicola is a teacher. I think they'd like a family, but there are no signs of it as yet.'

Annie was a wonderful source of information on the Cordells, and any facts Alex gleaned now would help her have a more comfortable evening with strangers.

The next pressing task was what to wear. In the end she decided on a plain black dress with three-quarter sleeves. It had a slim skirt and the upper section flattered and skimmed her figure. She brightened it up with a colourful silk scarf, draped casually around her neck and brushed her hair until it shone like copper.

Taking more time than usual with her make-up, when she finally studied her reflection in the mirror, she was satisfied with the results and she felt confident as she made her way to the dining-room, where she could already hear the sound of muted voices.

The visitors had arrived that afternoon, she'd seen them walking with Julian in the garden, but she kept out of the way to give them a chance to catch up on family news without her presence. Entering the dining room she found that they were already seated at the table.

'Ah, Alex! Come and meet my brother, William, and his wife, Nicola.'

Julian was wearing a white shirt and conservative tie. Alex thought that he had a polished veneer about him that only came from assurance and self-confidence. She shook hands, and returned their smiles before she sat down.

Julian regarded her for a moment, before he asked, 'Sherry?'

She nodded, and he poured her a glass from a decanter standing on the sideboard next to a silver dish containing shiny red apples.

Annie was right, the two men were not alike, but there was something in the way William described their journey from a village near Reading that reminded Alex of Julian; he had the same kind of eloquence. William was a few years younger; he was tall and loose-limbed. His wife, Nicola, was lively; her laughter was spontaneous and bubbled over. William was steady whereas Nicola viewed life with light-hearted friskiness. They complimented each other's characters. William viewed his wife with indulgent but obvious affection.

William asked Alex, 'What do you think of Cumbria, Miss Paxton? Julian mentioned you come from near the Welsh Borders.'

'Call me Alex, please! There's no comparison.' Alex licked her lips and wondered why she was so nervous. 'The countryside at home is not so rough, not so wild, but I like it here very much. Even though it's not a gentle kind of beauty, it's still lovely in a very special way.'

'Umm! I agree. Some people find it's too harsh, especially in winter, but I like it just because it isn't so tame and so polished.' He looked across at Julian. 'Julian and I spent several school holidays hiking along various British coastal pathways in our youth, didn't we, Julian? Remember the west coast-line of Scotland? That was fantastic! I wasn't surprised when Julian bought this place and decided to settle here. These kind of surroundings appeal to him, and to me too. Nicola and I usually spend our holidays in places that are a bit wild. Last summer, we wandered through some pretty unin-habited areas in the Spanish Pyrenees.'

Nicola joined in. 'It would be more appropriate to use the term uninhabited and isolated.' She smiled infectiously at Alex. 'He delights in taking me to places where I often wonder if we'll come out alive!'

'Where did you stay?' Alex asked.

William was still telling her about where they'd been, and what they'd seen, when Annie started to serve the meal. It felt strange to have Annie around only in the role of cook and housekeeper, but she clearly felt com-pletely happy — and one mouth-watering course followed the next.

The conversation flowed and Alex caught tit-bits about Julian, about their mutual acquaintances and about past happenings. When Annie brought the coffee in, everyone praised her efforts. They moved to the sitting room.

Following the others down the corridor, she walked behind Annie carrying a tray loaded with the used crockery. She asked quietly, 'Can I help, Annie?'

Annie shook her head, looked at her gratefully, and said quietly, 'No, of course not. It's kind of you to offer, but this is my job, in the same way it's yours to type his books. It isn't often that Julian has visitors. Join the others and have a nice time.'

They sat around a crackling fire, listening to some classical music playing in the background. Alex had heard the same piece of music before. Julian often listened to music when he was working and this particular piece was clearly one of his favourites. The conversation continued along friendly paths. Sipping some cool white wine from a long-stemmed crystal glass, Alex listened and joined the conversation whenever appropriate. Julian made an obvious effort to include her as often as he could.

His features were animated and soft and he seemed pleased with himself, and surveyed her with approving eyes. Her feelings towards him were becoming confused, and his scrutiny sometimes disoriented her thoughts more than she cared to admit. She was glad Nicola liked chitchat. She stopped Alex from questioning her mental occupation about Julian.

'I'm really glad you're here, Alex. Alone with these two, the conversation this evening would have been male-orientated. They're making an effort for a change. When I'm on my own with them I sometimes think I'm invisible.'

Julian smiled. 'True! We're definitely not guilty of talking about all male themes either! Remember the last time you were here? We had a long discussion about fashion. I remember you were particularly interested in what kind of underwear they wore in the Middle Ages and earlier.'

In a bantering tone Nicola said, 'True, that was one time when the topic was interesting. You know I'm always curious about things like that. I don't care about who murdered who, but I am interested to know if they wore knickers!'

Alex laughed loudly.

Soon after she smothered a yawn and looked at her watch. Julian offered to refill her glass, but she covered it with her hand and stood up. 'Thanks, but I think that it's time for bed for me.'

'Already?'

Nicola noted the tone of his voice with mercurial sharpness.

Alex laughed softly. 'It's almost twelve o'clock.'

'Oh! Is it?' He paused. 'Goodnight! Sleep well!'

She smiled at him and then said a general, 'Goodnight,' to them all before she quietly left the room.

Nicola and William both said, 'Goodnight, Alex,' in unison. Nicola twisted the stem of her glass absentmindedly and followed Alex's departing figure with a speculative glance.

Upstairs Alex opened the window and leaned out. The stars were glimmering in a blue velvet sky. She hugged herself in the cool night air. The evening had been very enjoyable, and made her wish she could find an easy solution to some of the world's problems.

7

It was a beautiful spring morning. The air was sharp and fresh, and sunshine flooded the countryside. Alex had Josh at her side and was heading for the path at the back of the house, when she saw Nicola a short way ahead of her.

Nicola turned when Josh drew level, and she waited for Alex to catch up with her. 'Hi! Going for a walk with his majesty? Shame on me! I must admit I didn't think of Josh. Of course — he's probably desperate to have a decent run now and then, isn't he?'

'Umm! He races around like a mad thing for a while. It's hard to believe that the placid, peaceful creature we see in the house is the same one who runs out here.'

Nicola agreed with a casual nod. 'Isn't it lovely weather? William is reading the newspaper. I decided to leave him to it.'

Alex thrust her hands deeper into the pockets of her anorak and took a deep breath. 'Yes. After the miserable cold and dismal grey of winter, it's marvellous to feel the sun again.'

The pale honey coloured eyebrows arched mischievously. 'Come on, tell me — what's it like to work for Julian?'

As casually as Alex could, she answered. 'Interesting! In the beginning I thought we wouldn't get on; my first impressions weren't good, but when we actually started to work together we managed fine. I think we're used to each other now. He's a demanding boss, but fair. If you do your job properly he's happy.'

'Anyone could tell last night that Julian was happy with how you fit in here. I presume it wasn't easy for you. William is a stickler for details, and I think Julian is a bit of a perfectionist too. Julian is probably more demanding because of what the accident did to him, and his life.'

Alex laughed softly. 'It's probably a good thing to be a perfectionist, if you happen to be an author of specialist literature. If he gets it wrong, someone, somewhere, will notice. His professional reputation would collapse around him like a pack of cards if he wasn't accurate and on target.'

The sheep eyed them nervously as they passed, darting away from Josh when he drew level — even though he was on the lead again. Light breezes ruffled the women's hair, and their shoes left damp outlines on rough grass. The sun hadn't yet driven the wetness of the morning dew away. They climbed over a stile, and began to follow one of the well-trodden paths. It ran parallel with the wall where hawthorn trees had taken root here and there. They huddled in tight forms and the spring breezes tried in vain to rustle and disturb them.

Nicola broke the companionable silence. 'We're glad Julian is writing. It was a blessing in disguise that he still had that to turn to after Gillian's death. He withdrew into a shell for a long time after it happened, but then writing helped to pull him out of the abyss.' She stopped and faced Alex with a friendly expression. 'I'm sure you guess that we ask Annie to let us know how he is. Julian never says much on the phone. Without Annie we'd be completely in the dark about how he's progressing. Julian isn't the type of person who asks for help or support.'

Alex was pensive. 'Life is very unfair sometimes, isn't it? He's such a good writer, and I hear that he used to be a good lecturer before the accident too. It's a shame that he won't consider doing that again.'

Nicola shrugged her shoulders. 'Julian is Julian. He was always a law unto himself, even before the accident. He was someone who made up his own mind, an indomitable sort of person. Gillian was the only person who could wind him round her finger and make him change his mind. She was good at that.' Nicola was lost in her own reveries for a moment before she went on. 'He coped wonderfully with the inquest and all that. A lot of people would have gone to pieces.' She adjusted her scarf.

Nicola started walking again and Alex kept pace. 'What . . . what happened exactly? When I asked Annie she just said it was an accident. Keith Arden told me it was a car crash caused by black ice. I've hesitated to ask too many questions; it's not part of my job to be curious about my employer's private life.'

'Of course it is. You live in the same house, and work with him every day. It would be pretty unusual if you weren't curious about the situation.' Nicola shoved her hands deeper into her pockets. 'Julian met Gill at university. She was a willowy blue-eyed blonde. She had a lot of admirers, but then so did Julian.

'To give her credit she hung on his every word, and Julian was flattered. As soon as he was a junior professor, they married, and she forgot any ambitions she may have had before that. I never understood if she was intelligent enough to get a degree, why she didn't utilise it. She didn't even do anything practical to relieve him of some of the work involved on his books, although she was perfectly qualified to do so.

'She seemed to put all her time and energy into organising his climb up the ladder of success. She made sure he met all the right people, and made the right connections. She came from an affluent background; so all the socialising came naturally to her. Shall we sit down for a while?' Nicola indicated in the direction of a section of the wall that was crumbling. It provided an ideal seating place.

They made themselves comfortable, looking at a view that stretched from the sparse greenery across the fields to the far distant hazy hillsides.

'The accident happened four years ago in December. The roads were icy, and Julian wanted to stay home, but Gillian was determined to go to some cocktail party or other at one of the big hotels because an important publisher was attending. Julian was driving and the car went out of control on a bend; it slid into the path of an oncoming vehicle. The man in the other car was drunk; perhaps if he'd been sober there might have been a chance. On top of everything else, Gillian wasn't wearing a safety belt because she didn't want to crush her dress — it was a bad habit she had, and she and Julian had quarrelled about it several times. It was the only thing I ever heard them openly quarrelling about. She shot through the windscreen; her injuries were so serious that she died on the spot.'

Alex shivered involuntarily.

'When Julian woke up in hospital, she was dead and he was paralysed from the waist down. The police and everyone else told him it wasn't his fault, but he seemed almost glad that he'd been 'punished' for what had happened — that he was crippled. The situation improved after an ensuing operation. He graduated from a wheelchair to crutches. He must hate it; he enjoyed hiking and played a lot of tennis before it happened.'

Alex could imagine him doing so. 'It must have been a nightmare for him.'

'He was disgruntled and impatient for a long time; although to give him credit, he never intentionally took it out on other people. He wanted to be on his own, and I think that was because he knew he might lose his temper with one of us. He came back to Charter House. We kept an eye on him from a distance and visited him whenever we could. We relied on Annie, and still do, to keep us in the picture. I'm glad to see there's a noticeable improvement this time; not so much in his mobility but he's mentally more cheerful, and he looks better. Last night, it was almost like old times. Even William noticed the difference.'

'Perhaps it would have been easier to

cope with if they'd had children. It'd have given him something to live for, something to work for; perhaps even motivated him to grab the chance to improve his mobility.'

Nicola's voice was cold. 'Children were not very high on Gillian's list of priorities. She can't defend herself any more, but Gillian was too decorative and too self-centred to want a family. Perhaps I shouldn't say that, now she's dead? It's a sad fact that she was killed, but it doesn't stop me ignoring the truth. She and I never saw eye to eye about children. For me they are terribly important, for Gillian children were a nuisance.' She paused, probably wondering if she'd said too much, and looked a little uncomfortable.

Alex gave her a reassuring glance. 'I'm sure you're not being vindictive and it isn't wrong to say what you believe.'

Nicola sighed. 'William and Julian know I didn't hit it off with Gillian. We never quarrelled openly or anything like that, we just kept our distance and only had a polite interest in each other because we wanted completely different things from life.'

Alex nodded understandingly again.

'The topic of children was always like a red rag to a bull. William and I have wanted children from the word go, and it just hasn't worked out so far. Julian wanted a family too, I remember once him joking about none of the Cordells having children, and it was about time that we all did something about it. Gillian patted herself on the back every time we saw her; she told me that she had persuaded Julian to wait a bit longer.

'She supported him wonderfully in making his name as a writer, but when he was well known he seemed to bask in his success more than he did himself. She liked the publicity, the advertising jaunts, and the interviews. Children wouldn't have fitted into the kind of life she envisaged. I sometimes wonder if their marriage would have eventually run into difficulties. It takes more than public fame to keep a marriage afloat. Julian likes children; I've seen how he handles them, they like him and that's a sure sign. His books are important to him because it means people acknowledge his skill and knowledge, but to Gillian they were only a means to fame and the limelight.'

Alex nodded silently. She pushed the conversation gently in another direction. 'How long have you been hoping for a baby? You don't mind me asking?'

'No, of course not! It's got to the stage now that my colleagues know that it hasn't worked out again from the look on my face when I walk into the staff-room.' The accompanying laugh sounded hollow and unconvincing.

Alex's voice was sincerely sympathetic. 'You're not alone. My brother and his wife were in the same position. It took over seven years; they did all the tests, followed all the advice and treatment, and still nothing happened. They eventually decided to give up and applied for adoption. They were in the process of ploughing through the mountain of paperwork when it happened at last! My niece is now two. The doctors told them it wasn't unusual. When couples want a baby too badly, sometimes the mechanism blocks for no apparent reason. When they stopped worrying, and counting days, things righted themselves of their own accord.'

'The doctor at the clinic told me roughly the same thing; they can't find any physical reason why I can't conceive. It's awfully hard for me not to think about it all the time. Sometimes I'm scared it' going to damage our marriage.'

'You seem to be putting an awful lot of pressure on yourself. Try to face up to the fact that it might not happen. You have a good marriage, and that's special. My brother and sister-in-law were told to be grateful for their good relationship and concentrate on that. There's no point in making your life a hell, and putting your marriage in danger. If you get pregnant fine, if not, there's always adoption.'

'William keeps telling me to relax and think of something else, but it's hard.'

'There are self-help groups. You can talk to other women going through the same thing. I think my sister-in-law used to talk regularly via e-mail to someone. I'll ask her where she got the address if you like.'

'Why not. A chat with someone who really understands would help. I'll give you my e-mail address. Thanks Alex.' Her blonde hair swirled around her face in the wind and the sadness in her eyes faded slightly. She made an effort to return to normality. 'This weekend is turning out well as far as I'm concerned. I'm glad that we've met.'

Alex smiled back at her and looked at her watch. 'We ought to go. I suspect that Annie is already banging away at the pots and pans.'

'You can bet your bottom dollar on that! She spoils us dreadfully when we're here. Sophie is coming sometime this morning too. You've met her already I think?'

Alex nodded. 'It's a family day. I wanted to make myself scarce.'

'What nonsense! Julian has invited Dr Arden; he's not family. Is Annie matchmaking between you and Keith Arden by any chance — I wouldn't put it past her!' Nicola tilted her head to the side.

'Me? And Keith?' Alex laughed out loud. 'No, decidedly not. I like him, but I've no special interest in him. I'm glad to lean back and watch others at the moment.'

'Because you already have someone?'

Alex shook her head. 'I made a pretty stupid mistake, believing I'd met my knight in shining armour — but he was a wolf in disguise.'

'It's his loss, not yours, I'm sure!' She mused silently. 'Then Annie is matchmaking away between Sophie and Dr Arden. Hmm — not a bad combination come to think of it! That leaves you and

Julian left to even the numbers up, so you'll have to put up with him all day I'm afraid — she's clearly paired you off with Julian.'

'Don't be silly. She doesn't need to; we're together every day.' She laughed. 'I'd like to see Julian's reaction if he thought Annie was trying to manipulate him.'

Nicola jumped down from the wall and brushed down her clothes. She didn't answer, but she smiled back at Alex, and kept her thoughts to herself.

8

Alex typed determinedly, ignoring the urge to yawn. She paused after a while to look out of the small window at the back garden. Yesterday had been enjoyable; in fact it was a lot of fun. They all treated her as if she was a family friend, and although Alex was nervous at first, she soon felt completely at home with them, and the day progressed well. Sophie arrived soon after breakfast and Keith Arden came to tea. They were still all together after midnight.

Annie was in her element. After the evening meal, Sophie produced a game of general knowledge for them to play. They all protested feebly about playing kids' games, but a short time later everyone's objections were forgotten among shouts of laughter and loud remarks. It was a close thing. In the end Sophie won, with Julian a close runner-up.

Alex conquered the desire to chuckle, when she noticed Nicola staring pointedly at Keith and Sophie all the time. Julian watched them too, and his glance wandered more often than necessary in Alex's direction. His thoughts were disturbed. When they broke up, Keith offered to see Sophie to her car parked further down the lane, on his way home to his cottage.

William and Nicola had stayed overnight and left very early that morning. William was going to drop Nicola at her school, on his way to his own workplace.

Alex said her goodbyes to them last night. She now stared at a couple of birch trees in the corner of the garden; in the weak sunshine their leaves seemed to shimmer like silver coins. She longed to grab Josh and go for a walk; it would be nice to go through the memories of a pleasant weekend again before they finally faded away. She sighed and turned determinedly back to the work.

Julian surveyed her kindly across the desk as she handed him the typed pages a short time later. She felt very relaxed with him after the weekend; she knew he'd made a special effort to make sure she didn't feel left out. Watching him, as he studied the text, she was almost overwhelmed by a feeling of contentment, and the knowledge made her nervous.

She'd completely misjudged Tony and it was dangerous to give Julian too much thought. She'd burnt her fingers, and should have learned her lesson — if she ever found someone to love, he'd have to be dependable, his love unquestionable. Julian wasn't a flirtatious man and probably never had been; it was unlikely that he saw her as anything else than an efficient assistant. He was anchored in the past with the memory of his wife.

He looked up and nodded as he handed her the papers. 'Fine.' The warmth of his smile echoed in his voice. 'Let's have our coffee break in the arden. I don't know about you, but I need some fresh air.'

Alex agreed willingly and left the pile of typing on the hall table on the way to the kitchen.

When he came, the fragrant aroma of coffee was wafting in the air. He glanced around briefly. 'Where's Annie?'

'I don't know, but at a guess I'd say she's cleaning and restoring the guest room to its former pristine glory.'

His mouth curved into an unconscious smile, and her heart skipped a beat. 'Lead the way then. She'll join us if she wants to.'

Settled in the arbour, facing the sun, it was pleasant. Alex breathed deeply and cupped her hands around her mug.

He asked, 'Did you sleep well?'

She raised her eyebrows and the corners of her mouth turned up. 'Like a log, but for some reason I'm still tired this morning.'

He laughed softly. 'Yes, I know what you mean, partly because of that game. I thought it would never end. You must be used to late nights though; discos, that sort of thing?'

She blinked and felt a little light-headed. 'I'm getting too old for discos.' He chuckled without commenting. 'I never enjoyed them much anyway. I enjoy other things more.'

'Like?'

She took another sip. 'Cinema, concerts, a good meal in a restaurant, visiting places of interests, gardens, museums . . . that sort of thing. It was a nice day yesterday, wasn't it? I enjoyed Friday evening too. I like your family.'

'Umm! It was nice to see them all again and you fitted in without a hitch.'

Annie's voice interrupted them; her voice carried across the garden from the kitchen doorway. 'Alex . . . there's someone to see you.'

Alex was puzzled. 'Who?'

'Tony . . . Tony Taylor.' She paused. 'Do you want to see him?'

Alex answered quickly. 'Yes, show him in please, Annie.' She looked briefly at Julian. 'Is it all right with you?

It shouldn't take too long.'

He began to get up, reaching for the crutches. 'Of course, take your time!'

'Would . . . would you mind staying? I'm not scared of him, but I don't want to see him on my own any more, and he might leave sooner if someone else was present.'

He sank down back on to the wooden seat again. 'I'll stay, if it helps. But just give me the wink if you decide differently.' He picked up his mug and played absentmindedly with it.

Tony's elegant figure strode towards them in his usual bold and confident manner. Alex noticed how he looked around, assessing the surroundings as he progressed. She introduced the two men and they shook hands politely, weighing each other up. Tony saw the crutches and quickly concluded the other man was no competition. Alex knew Tony too well not to misunderstand, and her intention to remain calm crumbled.

She straightened her shoulders and

looked at him with a vague hint of annoyance. 'What can I do for you, Tony?'

He looked at Julian pointedly, but before he could utter a request for them to be alone Alex read his mind and cut him short. 'I want Professor Cordell to stay. Anything you have to say to me, you can say in his presence.'

Tony felt riled by the company of the other man, but he had to put up with it. He hadn't driven all this way in the hope for conciliation with Alex, to let it be spoiled by a man with crutches. He felt confident that he could persuade Alex to come back to him.

'I've some papers from the lawyers for you to sign.' He paused and tried to look remorseful. 'I realise I was a fool and I'm begging you to give me another chance. I never loved her in the way I loved you.'

Julian stared at Tony with stony eyes. He seethed with anger, but forced his attention away from this tall healthy man to study a dark brown root from a nearby tree that ran into the ground like a snake. Somewhere in the hedge a bird was singing. Julian was glad he had himself under control; he'd had lots of practice in the last couple of years.

Alex shook her head vigorously. Her cheeks were bright red. 'Save your breath! We've been through all this before. You should have stopped at home and sent the papers with the post. I hope my signature really finalises things between us. I don't expect much financial return from the work I put into the firm. It was only just beginning to show real financial returns when I left.'

He had the grace to look downcast for a few seconds after he met her eyes, but recovered quickly. He reached into the pocket of his jacket and handed her a folded document. She took it wordlessly and opened it. Her eyes skimmed the contents. She turned to Julian.

'Would you check it for me, please? It seems straightforward, but two heads are better than one.'

Julian was glad to have something to do. He took it and proceeded to go through the text. He looked at Alex; his voice was firm. 'Seems all right. As far as I understand, it cancels all business agreements or contracts between you two, and any that Mr Taylor might have made under your name since you left the agency. It also states you are not responsible for any deals made since your departure. This was already covered by a temporary agreement, so it seems. Do you trust these lawyers?'

'Hey! What are you talking about? Are you suggesting I am trying to cheat Alex out of something?' It was clear by the way he levelled his words at Julian and tone of his voice when he did so, that Tony resented the other man. The visit wasn't turning out well. Alex patently trusted this man more than she did him. He couldn't figure out if they had more than a business relationship going.

Alex was reacting like an iceberg, and

this Cordell was also reserved and clearly hostile. The man was her employer, but they seemed too comfortable in each other's company for his liking. Cosy mugs of coffee in the garden, weren't usually part of a business contract. The other man's presence annoyed him. Tony's resentment was growing; his anger was on the boil.

Julian eyed him calmly. 'I'm not 'suggesting' anything, Mr Taylor. Alex is entitled to protect her interests in whatever way she chooses. She asked me to check the text, and offer my opinion, and that's what I'm doing. I think it's quite normal for me to ask if she thinks the lawyers are trustworthy.'

The two men looked coldly at one another and Tony muttered something inaudible under his breath.

Alex rushed her answer. 'They're reliable, Julian; I know them. They wouldn't put their reputation on the line to do Tony a favour. The sooner I put this whole thing behind me the better.' She took the paper back from

Julian and put it on the table. 'Can I borrow your pen?' Alex knew Julian usually had one in his pocket.

Julian handed her it and she signed her name.

Tony was frustrated. 'So that's the way the wind blows, eh?'

Alex sighed. 'What do you mean, Tony?'

'As I see it, you are throwing aside a going concern and ignoring the chance for us to re-establish our relationship, to move in with another man on the rebound. What's he got, that I haven't?' He indicated with his head towards Julian. 'Apart from a pair of crutches!'

She glowered at him, hissing with fury and indignation. 'How dare you!' She thrust the paper at him with one hand, and slapped his face hard with the other. Her cheeks flamed and the anger was plastered across her face. 'You are utterly disgusting! I never realised how low you could sink. Get out! Get out of my life, and stay out!'

Tony was stroking the reddened area of his cheek. He bit his lip and felt ashamed of himself. His anger had got the better of him, but he still couldn't find enough courage to apologise on the spot.

Julian looked on silently, his lips thin and white with anger.

Alex was more than angry. 'I never realised that even though you were successful as a businessman, just how little you were worth as a man. I didn't intend to argue or discuss what happened any more, but just remember that I worked very hard to keep my side of the bargain. I was too busy working to notice that you were probably squandering our income on other women!'

'Only someone who acts so underhand and cranky, like you, could sink so low as to insult someone who is compromised through no fault of his own — someone you don't even know. For your information, you're not worth the ground he walks on.' She drew in a long breath and pointed briefly in the direction of the house. 'Get out!'

Tony reddened before he turned

abruptly without replying and hurried off as if the devil was at his heels.

Julian swallowed the lump in his throat. His voice brought Alex back to earth. 'Don't worry about what he said. It doesn't matter. He was angry at losing you, he just hit out.'

She felt the tears gathering at the corner of her eyes. 'Of course it matters! No-one should ever speak to you like that. It is horrible of him to hurt your feelings just to get some kind of cheap revenge on me. It was an abominable thing to do.'

He tried to produce a weak smile. 'Oh, Alex! Since the accident, I've heard so many unintentionally cutting remarks about crutches, or people with crutches — it doesn't bother me any more.' He shrugged. 'People are some-times thoughtless. This guy was trying to win you back. When he saw that he'd lost, in his frustration he let rip and I happened to be around.' He reached out and gave her hands a squeeze before he let them drop again. 'Don't let it worry you. Let's get some work done and forget him. I promised the first ten chapters by the end of next week.'

Alex nodded and smiled weakly, her brow still furrowed. 'You're right. He's not worth it. I'll get some fresh coffee; this is cold. I . . . I'm really sorry Julian. I didn't want to get you involved. I never realised he could be so mean.'

'Don't apologise, it's not your fault. I bet Annie is waiting to fill your ears with sympathy and words of wisdom. I'll be in the study.'

Left alone in the arbour for a moment, Alex didn't register how Julian's grasp tightened around the crutches and how the knuckles showed white or how he muttered quietly. 'Damn, damn, damn!' The muscles tightened over the jawbone. There was an expression of frustration on his face before he heaved himself to his feet, watched Alex's departing figure, and made his own slow progress back to his desk.

9

Annie asked her what had happened, and Alex told her. Annie's hand flew to her mouth when she heard how insulting Tony had been.

'What an awful man! Whatever did you see in him, Alex?'

Alex tried a weak smile. 'I wonder myself; I must have been blind.'

Julian didn't mention Tony's visit again, so she didn't either. The weather improved; now there were often balmy days with bright blue skies and lots of sun. The publishers wanted a rough draft of the book. Julian was forced to leave detailed polishing, to put the whole thing into a halfway presentable state. Alex watched his expression all the time when he wasn't aware of it. She couldn't understand why she was so drawn to him, and she tried in vain to resist thinking about him.

The church held its annual summer fete the following Saturday afternoon. The weather was perfect, with blue cloudless skies and pleasant temperatures. Annie entered for a couple of competitions, so Alex went along to give her support. She looked for the adjudication-tent. At the upper end there was a table. On it was a big assortment of various items of foodstuffs that were entered for the various competitions.

Women were fussing around with vases of flowers, pots of jams, and plates displaying cakes, tarts and pies. Alex smiled as she wondered if the judges were insured against wrathful losers. Alex watched as Annie was declared winner of the jam, and fruitcake competitions. Alex knew quite a few people by now, and felt pleased when they stopped to chat, or at least smiled and greeted in passing.

Flags and coloured bunting flattered in the wind, and the smell of grass and wild flowers drifted across the fields. To her surprise she spotted Julian at the edge of the field, leaning against the fence. She made her way towards him. 'Hello! I didn't know you were coming. I didn't think this is your kind of thing.'

He liked her loose dress dotted with its sprinkling of bright poppies, but kept silent. 'It isn't. Annie would never forgive me if I don't show up on the most important day of the year.'

Alex grinned and signalled agreement. 'She's already won two competitions. I expect a lot of the village women live in hope that she'll go down with flu one year!'

His answering smile was lazy and he watched her wedge herself next to him against the fence. The wind blew the dress's flimsy material across his legs. 'And just think! We get the benefit of her cooking all the time!' He paused. 'I'd have come anyway.'

'A special reason?'

'I'm a member of the organising committee — an honorary membership nowadays, but I used to help actively before the accident. The church tower needs repairing and we have to get the funds from somewhere.' He looked into the distance. 'Gillian was in her element for a couple of years, organising everything. I should tell them to take me off the list; I can't help much any more. They'd be better off having someone doing something tangible to help.'

Alex scuffed the ground with the tip of her shoe and studied the mark it had left in the grass. 'There are lots of things you can do, if you want to. Not everyone needs to climb up and down ladders or put up strings of lights. Someone has to invite someone to open it, inform the first aid services, get donations, or encourage people to give prizes. More effort goes on behind the scenes than anyone imagines. I wish you wouldn't harp on about your inability to do physical things, like you do. You manage extremely well and you know it. You could even enter a competition.'

He gave a throaty laugh and looked around. 'A competition? For instance?'

'What about the obedient dog competition?'

He burst out laughing, and his eyes twinkled. Alex was glad to see him so relaxed. 'With Josh?'

'Why not? He listens very well, and he is obedient. Don't pretend he isn't!'

'But you can imagine him surrounded by other dogs and lots of people?'

'If you took him through the routine a couple of times he'd behave beautifully. He likes showing off, haven't you noticed?' She ignored the amusement in his eyes.

'What about a cup of tea?' She straightened up, and reached out her hand. 'The tea-tent is just over there and you dare not refuse. Annie is in charge of the tea-urn!'

He looked up at her for a moment and was silent, before he took her hand and let her pull him upright. He adjusted the crutches under his arms and increased the swing of his legs to keep pace with her as they crossed the field. A couple of minutes later he was seated with his long legs hidden under the table, and a generous piece of chocolate cake on his plate. There was a spicy smell from the carnations in a vase in front of them.

She noticed that various people stopped to chat to him and she intentionally vacated her seat at his side to encourage others to stay for a while. She wandered outside again.

'Hello Alex! Glad to see you.'

Alex smiled. 'Hello, Vicar. It's a good turnout isn't it?'

'Yes, it's a pity that more young people don't come — but that's how things are these days. They'd rather sit in front of their computers.' He paused. 'I saw Julian. I'm glad. He's had a bad couple of years and shut himself out of village life. You know about the accident of course?'

'Yes. He finds it very difficult to live with sympathy. He's a very independent personality.'

'You have had a good influence on him. He's a lot more cheerful. The mere fact that he came today is a very good sign, don't you think? Pity that you won't be staying.'

'Oh.' Alex was at a loss for words for a moment. 'I'm sure it has nothing to do with me. Just a natural development; time really seems to help to heal sometimes.'

The vicar made a vague movement with his hands. 'Don't underestimate how much you have helped him, my dear. It does him the world of good just to have another person around, some-one from outside, and from what he says, you are also very honest with him and he needs that too. Most people try to pretend his crutches don't exist because they don't want to hurt his feelings, but I think that just makes him feel worse.'

She kept her voice level. 'Yes, I know. He's very sensible, but I just try to think how I would react in the same situation. I think the only way is to be honest with him. Talk about the situation as far as he'll allow, and try to react normally.'

He nodded and patted her arm. 'You're right, and you are helping Julian. Oh dear! There's Mrs Prothero heading his way . . . Excuse me, Alex, but I must get away. For some reason she has singled me out to complain that her dratted seed cake didn't win one of the competitions. I'm going to seek some protection in the company of Dolly Wilson. She and my wife run the Women's Union.'

Alex laughed softly as he hurried away to be lost in the crowd. She didn't know Mrs Prothero, but she must be quite a formidable person. She bought a couple of items she didn't really need from one of the stands, and knew they would probably end up neglected and forgotten. She met Keith Arden at one of the stalls and helped him chose some knitted gloves and matching scarf. They were in gaudy stripes of red, green and yellow, and as they walked away from the stall, they looked at each other and broke into spontaneous laughter.

Alex looked up into his face and smiled.

Keith said, 'I know; they're quite awful, aren't they, but they looked so neglected. Perhaps I can get away with never wearing them. Trouble is, whoever knitted them, may have seen me buying them, and keep an eye out for them.'

'They're so bright, people will even see them in the dark.' Alex broke into laughter again, and wiped a tear from the corner of her eye. 'Oh dear! We're being horrible. Someone worked hard to make them. I can just imagine you wearing them next winter!'

Across the field at the entrance to the tea-tent, Julian watched them, unaware of why they were laughing, only that they were enjoying each other's company. His grip on the crutches tightened.

Alex left Keith circulating the field and took a short cut through the churchyard where the hummocks of the graves threw shadows on the green grass. She wandered down the lane and let herself in to Charter House. It was a rare feeling to find the house empty. She went to enjoy the luxury of a leisurely bath.

Later she heard the television in the sitting-room when she was on her way to make some tea. She looked in. Julian was watching a cricket match. 'So, you're back again too?'

He looked up and he caught the fresh perfume of the bath salts she'd just used. 'Yes, you can only eat a certain amount of chocolate cake. I think I'm going to burst.'

'You shouldn't be so greedy!'

'I can't resist it.'

'Cheesecake is my particular down-fall, but don't you dare tell Annie!'

He grinned at her and she smiled back.

'Like some tea? I was just on my way to the kitchen.'

'Sounds like a good idea.'

Alex carried the loaded tray into the sitting-room and sat companionably opposite him reading a magazine about someone's memories of their first love. The commentator's voice droned on; Julian found that his thoughts were not concentrated on the progress of his favourite cricket team. His glance wandered in her direction and he noticed she was laughing softly to herself.

'What's so amusing? Or is it something private?'

'No, not a bit. This article started me thinking about my first serious boyfriend. His name was Ken.'

'And?' Julian waited patiently.

'Oh nothing special, a very boring and banal story. I fell for him without knowing he was engaged. He didn't enlighten me, or try to dissuade my interest. My mother found out by chance I was following him like a sick cat all the time and bent his ear for not giving me the push! I was seventeen.'

His grey eyes appraised her with

interest. 'And I suppose you vowed never to forgive her?'

Alex laughed softly. 'Well, I didn't for a couple of weeks. I fantasised with the idea that he'd give up his fiancée for me, but he didn't of course.' She looked rather embarrassed. 'It sounds like I have a habit of choosing the wrong boyfriends, doesn't it? I have met some very ordinary nice men in my life as well though. Sorry! I didn't mean to bore you.'

'Nothing to do with you is boring, Alex.'

A shiver of pleasure went through her.

He continued. 'We all face our own failures or mistakes along the way.'

Her brow lifted. 'You? I can't believe that you've had many failures?'

'The usual kinds and to be honest, I think my wife thought I was quite a failure.'

Alex was taken aback, and indignant. 'Why would she? You're a well-known writer and you also had a successful academic career.'

He shifted and leaned forward. 'I'm only guessing, and I'll never be certain, but I sensed in her eyes she was unable to make head or tail of the fact that I didn't hanker after the prize-winning, the glamour of fame, the glitzy kind of existence that she loved. She wanted to make me a kind of super author of the century, and when she noticed I was resisting, her frustration spilled over into our personal relationship. If I'd dampened her ambitions early enough, perhaps her attitude would have changed.' He ran his hand across his face

Alex felt flattered that he'd been so honest with her. 'Without knowing what your wife was like, and not meaning any offence, I don't believe that you can change a person's basic character; it's not a good idea, is it? You can try to round off the corners perhaps, but that defeats its own purpose, doesn't it? If you try to change a person, you're trying to make them into another kind of person than the one you respected and loved.'

Silence fell between them then Julian said, 'I think you may be right. I couldn't have changed Gillian any more than she could have changed me. I was always passionate about my work and my writing, that's what was and is important as far as I am concerned. Gill viewed it as a step to another kind of life. We both thought we could live with the resulting differences.'

She nodded, and wondered why Gillian had never done her utmost to appreciate what was really important for Julian. Alex had the feeling as she watched him that the gap between them had closed a little. She decided it was time to change the subject.

The following Monday, without comment, Julian handed her a note he'd received from Tony with an apology for his 'ill-mannered remarks'. Her hair fell forward as she read the text. And her colour heightened.

'Well, at least he had the decency

to realise that he was extremely rude to you. It doesn't change my opinion about him.' She handed it back, and Julian crumpled it before he threw it into the waste-paper bin.

10

Julian's forehead was covered in lines, as he sat studying some of the typewritten pages.

Alex was sorting through some previously completed work on a side table. She was familiar with his facial expressions by now, and knew something was bothering him.

'Something wrong?'

He looked up, and his expression softened. 'No, not really. I was just thinking how many references in this particular chapter were at my fingertips in the university library, and how much time I'll have to spend searching through the internet to find confirmation.'

'Then why don't you just go to the university for a few hours and check them out? Or aren't you allowed to use the library any more?'

He was quiet for a moment. 'No, that wouldn't be a problem.' He went on. 'But I haven't done much driving since the accident. I've tried, but too much pressure on my left hip sets it off, if the journey is longer than a couple of minutes.'

Alex sighed, a little exasperated. 'Have you ever thought about getting an automatic car? You only need your right leg for that, there are only two pedals in an automatic!'

He smiled a little sheepishly and looked up into her face. 'You're right! Alex, I have never thought about that!'

She nodded briskly, and took a more solid stance. 'Men! Well it's time you did — you'll get a good price for your car in the garage; it looks brand new, and as far as I know it's been standing there unused since I arrived.'

He stared without expression into thin air. 'It was Gillian's car. There was no reason to keep it, but after the accident, I never got round to selling it. Mine was a complete write-off of course . . .'

Alex flinched and felt sick about raising the ghosts of the dead again.

He went on. 'William had mine scrapped when I was in hospital.' He ran his fingers through his hair; it sprang back neatly into place. 'It took a bit of self-control to get in Gillian's and drive the thing months later, but somehow I managed. Trouble was, even after I got over my misgivings, I found that driving wasn't as comfortable or easy as I hoped, so I more or less gave up. I have used it to go somewhere nearby in bad weather though, but not very often. I never thought about getting an automatic; that's the solution! Clever girl!'

Alex coloured slightly with pleasure. She fished around for a further diversion from the subject of Gillian. 'Would you like me to drive you to the university? If you think it would save you so much time, it would be worth a trip, wouldn't it?'

Julian had had a disappointing morning, work-wise, and the prospect was enticing. He gave her a measured look. 'You wouldn't mind?'

Grey eyes and green eyes locked. 'No, of course not!'

'Good! Then I'll say 'thanks' and take you at your word. When?'

'How about now?'

'Now?' He threw back his head and laughed.

Alex prised at the chink in his amour. 'No time like the present! If we leave straight after lunch, you'll have the whole afternoon to do your research.' She tilted her head to the side and said with easy charm. 'And it gives me a legitimate excuse to waste my employer's time, and go window-shopping for a few hours!'

On their arrival, she went all the way with him; right into the library, so she'd know exactly where to collect him again. He seemed a little uneasy at first when he caught the curious expressions of bustling students who made a wide berth around them as they moved along, but by the time they reached the silent sanctuary of the book-filled room he seemed more comfortable again.

While Alex was still looking around at the extensive surroundings when a voice cut through her thoughts.

'Julian? Julian? Good heavens! It really is you!'

A red-headed man wearing out-of-date, shapeless flappy clothes, and carrying an arm full of perilously piled books, hurried towards them. He automatically grasped for Julian's hand. Julian had to quickly transfer one crutch to a safer position in the crook of his arm, but his face split into a wide smile as he gripped the outstretched hand tightly.

'Bill! Great to see you! How's the history department? Still producing the best of the best?'

The man pushed his glasses further up his nose, and quickly adjusted his load to stop it toppling over on to the floor. In a slightly hushed voice he said, 'It's the same seventh world wonder it was in your day. You won't believe me, but Michael was asking me if I'd heard from you only yesterday. Strange, you turning up like this today. I could only tell him you'd ignored my letters and shut yourself away like a hermit.'

Julian shifted his weight uncomfortably, and looked uncomfortable too. 'Sorry, Bill! Nothing personal! I know that I should have made an effort, but it was all too much at the time. Thanks for your letters, especially the one you sent directly after the accident.'

Bill brushed his words aside with his free hand. 'You should have got in touch later though; we all expected you to come back eventually.'

'These . . . ' Julian lifted one of the crutches. ' . . . seemed an insurmountable hurdle.'

'Nonsense! What difference do they make to us, or to your work? Your brain is still intact! Your students missed you badly, and most of them vainly lived in hope that you'd come back before it was time for them to graduate. I was glad to see you kept busy with writing

your books though; jolly good too
— I've read them all!'

Julian was suddenly aware of Alex
standing silently at his side.

'Oh, Bill — this is Alex. She drove
me here today.'

Bill gave her a ready smile. 'Pleased
to meet you, Alex!' His attention
returned to Julian. 'I say, I'm free, and
Wallace is free too — I just saw him
walking, head down unaware of his
surroundings as ever, towards his study,
I'll see if any of the others are free. We
must have a chat, now that you've
finally found your way back! We need to
catch up on things!'

Weakly Julian started to protest.
'Actually, I came in to check up on
some sources for a new book, Bill!'

'Pooh! You can do that another time,
not now. No excuses! It's your own
fault for not coming in earlier! I'll just
see if I can find some of the old crowd,
meet you in my study in ten minutes
old chap! I've a very good Scottish
whisky and you can have the leather

armchair by the fire! It still smokes, when the wind comes from the wrong direction, but it's not surprising, these old buildings are a rule unto themselves!'

Julian laughed out loud. 'You'll never change, Bill!'

Bill obviously agreed, and grinned. Looking at Julian and addressing Alex, he said, 'You're welcome, Alex, too, of course!'

Alex smiled and knew Bill was just being polite. He was clearly looking forward to a man's 'thing'. She liked him on sight though; because she had the feeling hc was capable of achieving what a thousand well-meant words from others wouldn't. Fate must have put him here at this moment. 'That's very kind of you, but I'm sure you can manage perfectly well without me.' She looked at Julian. 'Julian has my mobile phone number. I'll come back whenever he's ready.'

When she did pick him up some hours later his grey eyes were lively, and his expression relaxed and pleased. He smiled broadly as she drew nearer. He didn't even sound regretful when he said, 'I'm afraid I haven't done any research.'

Alex nodded. 'I didn't think you would. But you seem to have enjoyed your reunion?'

He looked thoughtful for a moment, but then his mouth creased into a soft smile again. 'Yes! Yes, I did! It was almost like I'd never been away!'

'I'm glad!' Alex meant it.

'I'm afraid that, if you don't mind, you'll have to chauffeur me in to do that research on another day! Perhaps I can get some offers for an automatic car at the same time on the way — at the dealer I used to favour?'

'Oh dear!' She pretended to look apprehensive.

He was surprised, and it was audible in his voice. 'Is . . . is there something wrong?'

'There's a sale on at Debenhams, and I saw a very pricey outfit I liked, but resisted. I think I won't stand a chance, if it's still there when I go back a second time!'

They looked at each other and broke into spontaneous laughter. Julian reached out and squeezed her hand before he let it drop and they moved on. Alex thought the world was a pretty rosy place.

Back at Charter House, Alex parked the car at the front. She took the keys out of the starter, and got ready to get out. To her surprise, he leaned forward and gave her a quick kiss on her cheek. 'Thanks, Alex! Today wasn't any part of your contract.'

Alex was lost for words for a second and had an impulse to reach up and brush her cheek where his lips had touched. She didn't; instead she said, 'You're welcome!' She opened the door and slid out, reaching into the back seat to retrieve her bag. Julian had joined her by then, and together they went up the path to the rose-covered porch.

Alex was happy with the way they were getting on and didn't look too far into the future. The weather improved, and the temptation to go a little further grew with every passing day — especially if she could go with Keith. He got into the habit of looking for her if he went on a ramble. Alex was glad of his company; he was a comfortable person to be with.

Julian noticed they seemed to be together often, and he had a feeling he was getting to be an old and spiteful man. He flipped quickly through the paperwork lying within reach, to give himself something to do, or he just perched nervously on the sofa watching TV until he heard her come in again.

He asked no questions, but was quiet and almost abstract in his manner at such times. There was no smile from him when he saw the colour in her cheeks, and the brightness in her eyes. He felt more jealous than he had ever been in his life; it wasn't a happy experience for someone like him. It was also more difficult because he happened to like Keith.

When Keith called he changed the subject quickly whenever Alex's name cropped up in their conversations. He couldn't bare the thought that another man knew her better than he did.

On the work front, they made good and steady progress as the weeks passed; they were a good working team.

One day, on her way back to her room, loaded with some finished laundry, she almost bumped into Julian and Keith coming out of the sitting-room. Keith's eyes lit up and his smile followed immediately. Julian's expression was more reserved and his eyes were speculative as he stood listening to Keith.

'The woman in question! I've just persuaded your employer to sponsor you in our walk on Saturday in aid of the local hospice!'

Alex's chin dropped, and her mouth opened. 'You've done what?' She looked from one to the other.

Julian contributed a hesitant and un-helpful, 'Only if you want to, of course!'

Alex had to wait for Keith to paint the details. 'Our local hospice needs funds and all the local doctors and chemists organise a walk once a year. The hard part is to find sponsors of course!'

Still rather bewildered she said a breathless, 'Oh, I see! And what makes you think I can make any money? I'm not an athlete of any standing; I just enjoy walking for pleasure. You know that!'

Julian observed their obvious camaraderie and remained silent.

'You don't have to walk the length of a marathon! You only walk for as long as you feel comfortable, and there is no limit on time. You earn one pound per mile. The course starts at the church, goes along the common to Percy Wallace's farm, then round the old quarry and back to the church. That's roughly a mile. We just all go round in circles all the time.'

Julian noticed how her eyes twinkled and he watched the other man's happy face.

'As I'm part of the so-called committee, I'm desperate to get as many
people in on it as possible. I just
thought of you as I was talking to
Julian. Every single pound helps!' His
voice had a pleading tone. 'Oh! Come
on, Alex!'

She didn't hesitate for long. 'OK! I'll
let you twist my arm. I'll do my best
keeping the reason for this madness in
mind. I'll collapse after a couple of
rounds I expect!'

'Great! Every single participant helps,
and every single pound does too.'

'Who's sponsoring you?'

'Stan Bennett, at the petrol station!'

She nodded, and turned to Julian.
'You know that this is your own fault,
for not refusing don't you!'

Julian held her glance. 'I'll take that
chance. I hope you'll make me sorry I
agreed to sponsor you!'

Keith placed his hand lightly on her
shoulder, a gesture Julian didn't miss.
His lips tightened.

Keith looked down at her. 'Start is

nine o'clock, outside the church, no matter what the weather is like. Comfortable clothes, most suitable shoes you've got, and there will be drink provided along the way!'

'OK! I'll be there!'

Keith nodded in satisfaction, and Julian looked down at the tips of his shoes.

Saturday afternoon, she returned footsore, and very tired, but fairly satisfied with her effort.

Unconsciously Julian had been waiting for her return. He came out to meet her in the narrow hallway. The sparse lighting hid his face in the shadows. 'Well? How much do I owe you?'

'Ten, nearly eleven rounds; so you'll have to fork up ten pounds!'

She looked extremely attractive, despite the fact that she must be tired. Her skin glowed with the exercise.

'That's good. Well done!'

Her answering smile was wide, spontaneous and generous. He continued, 'I'll round it up to twenty!'

'That's generous, Julian. Thanks!'

He brushed her words aside. 'How much have they collected?'

'Someone said it was a couple of hundred already, so they'll be pleased.'

He nodded. 'You'd better get a shower! You'll catch a cold talking to me.'

11

What had gone wrong? Somehow there were new and invisible barriers between them, put up almost overnight so it seemed. At first Alex thought it was her imagination, but finally she had to admit that their tentative nearness was disintegrating before her eyes. She knew him well enough now to know that he'd deliberately hid himself and his feelings away from her. It was almost like the very first days in the job.

Alex tried to ignore it and searched for a logical explanation, a solution. She never forgot that he might be in pain and wondered if it was that for a while. Then she conjectured she'd done something to annoy him, so she just spent less time in the living-room in the evenings. When she did, their conversation was usually clumsy and artificial. Alex didn't understand him at all any more.

During working hours he used the cover of the book to keep their conversation on a smooth safe path. Outside office hours he withdrew, and although Alex tried hard to return to the relaxed relationship they'd shared previously, she felt he was intentionally blocking her attempts.

Even Annie noticed and asked Alex what was wrong. Alex could only shake her head. 'Nothing I know of, but perhaps he's in pain, and just won't admit it?'

Annie nodded and lifted her eyebrows. 'Could be. Perhaps Sophie, or Dr Arden, has been goading him about that operation, and he's irritated. He's fine with me, but there's something wrong. Is he short-tempered with you?'

Alex shook her head decidedly. 'No, not short-tempered, but I know what you mean. He's not a moody man by nature, but now he's withdrawn and distant.'

Annie eyed her speculatively, and her brain toyed with some thoughts she'd been having lately. 'Best leave him alone — he'll come round eventually.'

Alex nodded thoughtfully.

Alex was glad she could hide her thoughts behind the task of getting the book finished and tried not to observe him too carefully. Thank heaven he behaved quite naturally in the office. If she caught him looking at her too often with a disconcerted expression, or hurrying unnecessarily through explanations, she put it down to the pressure of work and ignored it.

Alex was often glad to go for a long walk at the end of the working day — to get out of the house and to be alone. She was in a quandary; some days she longed for the job to end, some days she found it hard to imagine being anywhere else than in this house. She began to realise there was a lot to be said for going home from the office at the end of the day; then you didn't have to face your silent employer across the dining table later in the day. She had to admit that for some reason it was impossible to ignore Julian Cordell, although she tried hard to fix her thoughts elsewhere and remind herself that Charter House would one day be a thing of the past.

'That was a lovely meal, Annie, thank you! I'll help you with the washing up when I've finished this trifle!' Alex smiled at the housekeeper.

Annie looked benignly at her. 'Oh no you won't! That's my job! Off you go. There's a very good film on the TV this evening, the papers are full of it. You're going to watch it, aren't you?' Her question was directed at Julian.

Alex didn't fancy sitting in the same room as Julian. It was good to notice he was still acting quite normally with Annie, and that he used the same kind of teasing tone with her, but it also depressed Alex even more because she was convinced she'd offended him in some way.

He pushed his empty plate away. 'Annie — that was great. You know I love your casseroles and I've had two portions, but I can't manage trifle on top of that.'

Annie turned a deeper shade of pink. 'Oh, go on with you! It's my job. I'll leave the trifle in the fridge, perhaps you'll feel like some later?'

Julian laughed. 'You never give up do you, Annie? If the both of you don't mind, I want to catch the early news.' Annie and Alex gave non-audible signs of consent and he got to his feet, hitching the crutches under his arm with accustomed skill.

Alex lay on her bed and stared at the ceiling. A book lay open and unread at her side. She folded her hands behind her head and decided the only thing she could do was to force the work as much as she could. They were on the final part of the book now anyway. She had come to believe that the sooner she could close the door on this episode of her life, the better.

She felt at home and comfortable with Annie, but Julian avoided personal conversations and kept his remarks curt and to the point. Somehow she felt hurt and upset. It would have been sensible to confront him but why did it matter? He was only an employer, and the contract was only a temporary one.

Their shared meals grew more silent. If Annie hadn't been present to lessen the tension with her talk of local news, Alex would have preferred to go to the local fish and chip shop or the pizzeria, rather than be forced to spend time with someone who clearly didn't want her company — even if he appreciated her working skills. Alex was looking forward to the time when she could leave.

Just a few weeks ago Alex thought he was an amusing and interesting man, someone with a wealth of general knowledge on all kinds of subjects and she always enjoyed being together with him. Now she was glad that they were nearing the end of the contract and she didn't want to analyse the situation too deeply. Ignore it, and get on with the job; it would all come to an end soon.

One afternoon when Alex was in the kitchen, she heard Julian shouting in the garden. It was very unusual, in fact she could only remember the one time when he and Sophie had been arguing about a new operation. She wondered what was wrong and went to the door to see what was happening.

Julian was leaning on his crutches and looking down at a little girl. Alex recognised her as the youngest of a family living a little further down the lane. Marnie stood like a drooping flower, a coloured ball clasped to her chest, and listening to Julian's loud reproaches.

'How many times have I asked you not to play near the fence, Marnie? I explained about the damage ballgames can do. Next time I'll keep your ball. Why don't you play at the bottom of the lane, or go to the playground? Why are you making a nuisance of yourself outside my house?'

The little girl was clearly frightened and close to tears. As she looked up her eyes were wide and her eyelashes glistened with unshed tears. 'I'm sorry, Mr Cordell! It won't happen again, promise.'

Julian adjusted his weight. 'If it does, you won't get another chance, I'll — '

Alex waited no longer. She hurried to crouch next to the little girl, and put her arm around her shoulder. 'Hello! You're Marnie, aren't you?' The little girl nodded. Alex smiled at her reassuringly, before she turned her gently in the direction of the open gate. 'Off you go, and I'm sure you'll be more careful in future.'

The little girl was unmistakably relieved. She nodded and clutched the ball more tightly. Outside Alex noticed there were two other older children, looking alarmed and waiting for Marnie. Alex gave her a gentle push and she ran off. The gate made a soft clank as the handle fell into the lock.

Alex straightened up and turned to him. There was a stony expression on his face, and his eyes were dark and unfathomable. She felt annoyed about the situation, and all the recent frustration rose to the surface before it finally spilled over.

'What on earth is the matter with you? A little girl loses her ball in your garden and you make an abominable fuss like that? Do you dislike children so much, or are you just being generally detestable?'

He stared at her without speaking; his expression empty. She noticed that his jaw-line tightened.

Alex raged on. 'For heavens sake! This is only a garden, an ordinary one like millions of others. There is not a single plant or flower that is worth frightening that little girl. Do you honestly think she lost her ball on purpose? Have you forgotten what it's like to be a kid? Did you never knock a ball into a neighbour's garden?' She looked around briefly and said point-edly. 'Did she actually damage anything in your precious garden?'

His lips were a straight line. 'I think

this is my concern, not yours, Alex. If I choose to tell her off it's my business and not yours!'

'It may not be 'my concern' as you put it — but that doesn't mean that I won't pass comment . . . because quite honestly, I find your attitude is pretty deplorable. I don't understand you, and I probably never did.'

'It's not your job to understand me. I don't want you to understand me, that's not what you're paid for.' His voice was cold and stiff. 'It's your job to type my book for me, nothing more and nothing else. I don't need you to tell me how to behave.'

Alex's colour rose to match her temper. 'That's a pity, because I'm coming to believe that you badly need someone to remind you that you are not the centre of the universe and that you have no reason to be nasty to a little girl for such a trivial mishap. You've lost your wife and part of your mobility, but that's no justification to make other people suffer because of it.

You could have another operation to improve your mobility, but you refuse to do so. You have to learn to accept the death of your wife, however painful it might be, because nothing can change that either.' She was almost out of breath.

His face was pale and he stiffened noticeably. Alex noted how his lips thinned and the skin on his cheekbones grew tauter. 'Thanks for your comments, Alex. I'll give them the attention they deserve. If you'll excuse me, I'm going for a walk now.' He whistled for Josh.

Alex turned on her heel. 'By all means! I just hope you don't meet up with any more children on the way — for their sakes as well as your own!'

She hurtled through the house and rushed up to her room, glad that Annie was out shopping. She didn't regret a word but knew it would make things worse and colour his attitude to her for the rest of her stay. When she reached her room, she stood looking at herself in the mirror.

She stroked her hair with hands that weren't steady and silently told herself it was impossible not to get emotionally involved about someone you loved. Her hands flew to her mouth and Alex held her breath. How stupid could you get! In love? She wasn't in love with Julian; she'd only just got over Tony! It was just her imagination, but was it?

One thing was sure; there was no future in loving someone who was so tied to his memories of another woman. She flopped down on to the bed and held her head in her hands. It was no use; she did love him. There was no logic in it; you fell in love with someone for what they were, not what you wanted them to be. Even with his complicated character, Alex had never met anyone she admired or respected more.

There were sides to him that were magical and charmed her, now and then they'd shone through the shield he'd built around himself. He'd coped with tragedy and sadness, and had come through it all to remain what he probably always had been — an attractive, interesting man to admire and respect. She'd been close for long enough to fall in love with him.

He'd never indicated that he saw anything in her other than an efficient secretary. She was really glad the book was drawing to a close — if she had to face some months and not just days, it would have probably been impossible to hide her hunger and longing for him. Now she'd pick an appropriate moment and tell him her next employer was waiting desperately for her.

The mood was businesslike and cool, and neither of them mentioned Marnie. Alex wished things were more comfortable, but she was glad they managed to keep going in a polite and businesslike way.

Without knowing why she'd had to do it, Annie told her that she'd bought a ball game and some chocolate for Julian, and he'd gone off down the lane to give it to Marnie and her brothers and sisters. Annie was peeling some onions at the sink.

'I know that he likes children, but why he suddenly decided he had to give them something is a mystery to me. I saw him talking to Bill, their father for a while and the two of them shook hands after. The kids were hanging on his jacket. It's a pity that he never had children of his own.'

Alex didn't comment. She knew why, but didn't explain to Annie; in effect he'd acted just as Alex hoped he would. Alex avoided talking about Julian to Annie; Annie noticed without commenting and wondered why they were both so blind. Alex avoided Julian's company as much as she could, making excuses to go for long walks. Keith met her often when he was out walking, and they often joined up. Julian viewed them with a gloomy expression from the window.

Alex watched television in her room in the evening, more than she'd ever done before. Finally the day came when she reckoned her part in the preparation of the book was finished. She printed out a final copy and put it on his desk.

It was a sunny morning. The birds were singing and their melody drifted through the open window. She swallowed hard, and avoided his face, as she had unconsciously been doing ever since the episode of Marnie. 'This is the complete print out.'

He nodded without looking up.

She took a deep breath to control her words. 'There's not much reason for me hanging about any more now, is there? If you do find mistakes, you're perfectly capable of correcting them yourself.' Was it her imagination, or did she see him flinch. He was still silent. 'You won't mind if I leave on the weekend? I have another assignment waiting, and my next employer needs my help as soon as possible.'

He looked up at last; his expression was empty, his body slightly slumped. 'No, of course; I won't keep you. As you say, the book is more or less finished. I can manage now.'

Alex took an unconscious small step back away from him and nodded. 'I'll clear the office tomorrow. If you find anything before I go I'll put them in, of course. I've already made a copy of the book in its present form, so in an emergency you always have a version as it is at the moment. Hereafter you only need to store adjustments each time, and when you decide to finally call it a day, I suggest you make at least two safety copies . . . one for yourself, one for the publishers, and then you can destroy this one.' She put a transparent plastic case on the desk; the sound echoed.

He picked it up and turned it in his hands. He nodded without comment or sign of any kind of emotion. She tried to offer him a weak smile, as a sign of goodwill. Her heart was beating wildly against her ribs. She turned and left the room. Julian picked up a sheet of paper, crumpled it into a tight ball and aimed it explosively at the fireplace.

Annie was a little surprised at the suddenness when Alex told her of her intended departure but she didn't comment too much, apart from that she'd miss her. Alex had intentionally mentioned it several times recently, but Annie had believed it was still too early to give up hope.

Alex would miss Annie, she'd miss Josh, but most of all she'd miss Julian. She couldn't imagine what it would be like not to see him again — but no-one would ever know that. She reasoned this was the inevitable end to an encounter with a man who meant more to her than anyone else in her life, but who hadn't noticed she existed in any other form than an assistant.

The wind was drumming showers against the window; and as the wind died away the sound of the steady rush of rain against the windowpanes was louder. At last came the empty silence. Lying wrapped in the warmth of her bed, staring open eyed through the darkness at the ceiling above, Alex didn't want to think about the moment of leaving but there was nothing else to think about.

When the time came, she hurried through her farewells. Her suitcase was packed in the hall, she knocked at the study door and went in. 'I'm off. I hope the book is a success and I wish you all the best for the future, Julian.' Her voice sounded stiff, but Alex was glad to be able to say anything at all. Her throat felt dry and tight. She held out her hand. He looked startled for a moment and he was pale in his face. He got up awkwardly and it reminded her of the day she'd arrived.

He took her hand and shook it. 'Thank you, Alex. Thanks for your help, and thanks for being so patient. What about a reference?'

'If I need one, I'll get in touch.' Alex vowed she never would; she had to break the bonds, not cling on to any strands of hope.

He nodded. 'Well, have a safe

journey, and take care of yourself.'

'I will. Say goodbye to your family, and to Keith next time you see him.'

She turned quickly and left the room, closing the door quietly behind her. She took several deep breaths, and fought back the tears that threatened.

Once she'd steadied herself, her farewells to Annie were mixed up in hugs and promises to keep in touch. Annie had her parents' address because Alex wasn't sure where the future would lead her. Annie had made her a huge packet of sandwiches, enough to feed an army; she also gave her a plastic container with a whole cheesecake.

She was unaware that Julian was watching from the window as she drove off.

The weather matched her mood. The sky was laden with heavy clouds that gradually began to send streams of rain on to the earth below. The cars in front threw up showers of water as their tyres ploughed the surface of the road. Alex drove as fast as safety allowed, and as the distance between Julian and her lengthened, she felt a growing sense of relief, mixed with a kind of despair.

It was the right thing to do; to prolong her stay would have only delayed the inevitable. It wouldn't have changed the ultimate result. She had her freedom again, and so did Julian; both of them should be happy. She wondered why she felt so desperately unhappy.

12

Alex spent a couple of weeks at home, but she was jumpy and nervous and needed something to divert her thoughts and her energies. She decided to look for work in London. It was far enough away and although she knew she wouldn't forget Julian, somehow she had to get some kind of purpose back into her life. The sooner she found something to occupy her time, and to relieve the strain on her bank account, the better.

She did sit down and write Keith a farewell note. They had spent a lot of time walking together, and her departure had been abrupt, without any goodbyes. She mentioned she was looking for a job in London and kept the contents chatty.

Applying for temporary posts advertised in the Sunday nationals, her qualifications and experience soon got her a job with a company of shipping agents. Just before she left for London with a couple of heavy suitcases, the postman handed her a letter. She saw it was from Keith and she read it on the journey. Alex was sure he had little time for personal activities, and she was touched to find he had replied so soon.

The letter was short and full of generalities. He missed their companionable walks and hoped that she'd visit the area again sometime in the future and call if she did. Alex didn't think that was very likely. There was no mention of Julian.

Alex threw herself into her new job and she was glad to work overtime. She was soon taking on more responsible work and had to be careful not to antagonise her fellow workers who were permanent members of staff. She sent Annie a postcard but without an address; she decided to let some more time pass and write her a letter with more information together with a Christmas card.

Her bosses were more than satisfied with her efforts and even offered her a permanent job, but three months on, Alex had already decided that nothing was easier than moving when you had no ties to hold you down. She'd already started to look for something abroad, and an agency had offered her the chance to work for a wine exporter in the south of France over the winter.

The prospect was tempting. Her French was passable, and as the firm was mainly interested in employing someone to handle the English side of their export business, Alex was sure she could cope. She had the contract in her bag, and was going to study it carefully over the weekend, before making a final decision.

Alex hurried from the underground entrance at the end of a day that had been hectic; she walked quickly along the last couple of hundred metres towards her rented two-room flat. She turned off the main road and the buzz of the busy traffic faded a little into the background. She reached the entrance to the cul-de-sac where she had taken the small flat for the duration of her stay in London.

She was deep in thought thinking about what she still had to do, and buy, before Sue and Stan came up for the weekend; an extra blanket and pillow for the couch in the living-room so that they could have her bed was at the top of her list. She strolled along the pavement. Railings bordered one side; behind them a small inner courtyard with flowers and small trees.

Now and then, the wind sent up clouds of leaves from fallen drifts under the nearby trees, lifting and spinning them up into the sky. The sun was hidden behind the houses, and it was cool. She shoved the thought of the coming winter to the back of her mind; in France it would probably be a lot milder than here. She scrabbled in her bag looking for her key, and was so deep in thought that she almost bumped into someone leaning on one of the pillars outside the block of flats.

He was wearing a dark navy wool coat, grey slacks and elegant brown shoes. The breeze ruffled his hair; it was slightly longer now than she remembered it, and she had a strong urge to reach out and touch him. He seemed almost unchanged; the same grey eyes, the same angular features, and the same lanky figure.

'Ju . . . Julian!' The surprise of suddenly seeing him took her breath away. 'What are you doing here?' Her colour faded completely as she studied him, and then her cheeks reddened again. She still couldn't believe it was Julian, but it was as if five months had been swept away in one glance. His tall figure and attractive features were so dearly familiar, and she was sharply aware how deeply they'd burned themselves into her memory. Looking at him now, she found she hadn't forgotten the tiniest detail.

He watched her and sounded almost apprehensive. His voice sent shivers down her spine. 'I got your address from your parents.'

His eyes mesmerised her and vaguely she noted that her mind was a crazy mixture of hope and fear. 'My parents?' she asked innocently. 'Why?' Now that the shock was fading a little, her emotions were under control again and she suddenly noticed that he was standing upright with a walking stick. Her voice heightened with excitement. 'You're walking without crutches? How wonderful! You finally made up your mind to have the operation?'

He looked a little self-conscious, but couldn't help smiling. 'Yes. Once the book was off my hands, I really started to think about what I wanted my future to be like. I decided it would be stupid not to give it a try, and after I'd considered things I thought I had a good chance. The surgeon explained everything in detail and said there was an excellent likelihood of success.'

'I went into hospital three months ago and it worked. I have some metal bits and pieces that will have to come out when the bones have knitted properly, but I'm almost free of pain now and I only need this to get around.' He lifted the walking stick. 'It's also temporary; the physiotherapist says if I keep doing all the exercises that it's only a question of time until I can throw it in the corner.'

Things were happening too fast, and happiness wedged in her throat like a lump. 'Oh! I can't tell you how glad I am. It must be wonderful to know that you'll be able to live a completely normal life again.'

He nodded. 'I wish I hadn't been so stubborn, and listened to Keith a long time ago.' He passed the walking stick from one hand to the other and watched her face. His jaw tensed noticeably as he said, 'He told me you'd written him a letter. I think Annie was quite jealous. By the way, he sends you his best wishes; he and Sophie are getting married at Christmas.' He studied her closely, watching how she took the news.

Alex's reaction was spontaneous. A smile of delight split her face. 'Really? That's marvellous! This really is a day for good news. Did you know that Nicola was speculating they might end up a pair, on that weekend when they visited you? I bet that she's patting herself on the back now.'

He hesitated and sounded almost relieved. 'You're glad?'

Alex was puzzled. 'Of course, why not? They are lovely people, and I imagine that they'll have a good and happy marriage, don't you? I hope so. I like them both.'

He looked awkward. 'I thought that you were very fond of Keith?'

The look of surprise spoke plenty even before she answered him. 'Keith? Of course I like him — because he's a very nice man. He's a good friend.'

He looked down quickly for a moment, before he searched her face again. 'I . . . I thought that when you were with us, that you and he were more . . . '

179

Something clicked in her brain; she knew what he was insinuating. 'That we were in love?' There was a slight tone of exasperation in her voice. 'Julian, I'd only just got over the way Tony cheated me when I came to work for you. Is it likely that I'd throw myself at the first man who crossed my path — however nice he might be?'

A muscle quivered at the corner of his mouth when he said, 'That would have been me not Keith, wouldn't it?'

She felt light-headed; the conversation was developing in a strange way. His expression was more cheerful now and Alex had to conquer her confusion, she even had a stupid desire to get up and run, because his presence was almost too much to bear. She'd believed she could forget him; seeing him standing in front of her, only proved how mistaken she was. She'd missed him terribly, dreamed of him, and constantly longed to see him again. She tried to put things back on a normal footing.

'You said you got in touch with my parents?'

'Annie reminded me the telephone number was probably on your application form for the job. She was right. Anyway, I phoned, explained who I was, and asked for your address. Your mother was very diplomatic. She didn't even ask why I wanted it, and gave it me straight away. She must be a very unusual woman!'

'I expect that she recognised your name, otherwise she might have asked questions. Does your visit have something to do with the book?' She couldn't think why else he would go to so much trouble to find her. 'Is there a problem? I'm more or less just about to agree to a job in France for a couple of months, but I still have a little time before I have to leave. I'll help if I can, of course.'

He shook his head. 'Nothing to do with the book. That's not due out for a while yet, but I've brought you a rough copy with the pictures included. I badgered them until I got one.'

He took a tidy bundle out of one of the capacious pockets of his coat and handed it to her. She took it and gripped it tightly. 'Thanks, and I'll look forward to buying the book when it comes out.'

His voice was almost a whisper and a muscle clenched along his jaw. 'I dedicated it to you.'

She looked at him in astonishment and her eyes widened as she stared at him in disbelief. 'You did what? Why? I was just a temporary employee.' She turned the first pages and looked for the acknowledgment. Her heart accelerated noticeably as she read, *To Alex with love. Without you I could never have completed this book — Julian*.

She swallowed a lump in her throat and searched desperately for something suitable to say. 'That's very kind of you. It's the first, and probably, the last time that anyone will mention me in their book. Thanks, Julian!' She tried to control the pages as the wind played havoc with them.

'If I'm lucky, I'll be able to mention your name in every book I ever write.'

It was hard to remain coherent when she was close to him, when she was mesmerised by him and by his words, and by the expression on his face. She was finding it increasingly difficult to remain sensible and aloof. 'Why should you?' Her heart was beating so loudly she was sure he must hear it.

'Because I'm hoping that I can persuade you to give France a miss. I'm hoping that you care enough for me to share the rest of your life with me. I'm hoping that you will grow to love me as much as I love you.'

She was breathless because she couldn't believe her ears. Her eyes searched his face trying to read his thoughts. In the end she managed to croak out, 'You love me? You couldn't even stand my company just before I left Charter House, and don't dare pretend otherwise.'

He relaxed a little and there was laughter in his eyes as he said, 'Yes, I admit it — or at least that's what it looked like to you, I'm sure. The truth is I couldn't bear the thought that you were in love with Keith. I couldn't bear the thought that other men were capable of living the kind of life I wanted to share with you. I went around like a bear with a sore head, and that's why I was so impossible. That's why I was so nasty to Marnie. I'm sorry Alex! I didn't want to hurt you! I don't know what was worse — living with you in the same house and not telling you how I felt, or losing you later, and missing you like hell ever since.'

She couldn't believe it. 'You really believed I was in love with Keith?'

He nodded and looked more at home with himself, now that he had begun, although he was still uncertain how she would react to his words.

'How could you be so stupid? Why didn't you give me a hint, ask me about him, or set Annie to find out? She's better than Sherlock Holmes at ferreting.' Her eyes sparkled as her instinct told her they were coming out of the dark.

'I was afraid to do that. I'm older than you. I've been married before. What could I offer you in comparison to someone like Keith Arden?'

'You were afraid? Of doing what?'

'Of revealing how I felt to anyone, especially you; I was afraid of hearing what I couldn't bear to hear — that you didn't care for me.'

She looked at him with unbelieving eyes. 'So you said nothing, and let me drift out of your life? You knew your injuries didn't matter. What has age got to do with it? I naturally wondered if you'd got over Gillian, but in the end I didn't need to because you shut me out completely and you were so cold and distant.'

She hesitated, but had to ask. 'What about Gillian? Can you honestly forget her? I can't take her place, Julian — I don't want to. I'm me, and I have no ambition to slip into her role. That wouldn't work, for me or for you.'

He looked surprised, but hope was rising in him; she hadn't rejected him outright. 'I don't want a replacement for Gillian if that's what you mean. I love you. You're unique and completely different; and there is absolutely no comparison. I swear that I will never compare you with her. I have never felt so at home with anyone in my life as I do with you. I could tell from the beginning that you accepted me as I was; you saw the person I was, everything else was secondary. You care, full stop, and I love you — everything about you.'

He added as an afterthought. 'Gillian disliked any kind of illness; and I often thought that she would have probably left me if she had survived, and I'd ended up as a cripple. I have no illusions about what Gillian was like. I don't think that it's important for you to know about her, but if you want to ask me questions, do. I'll try to be honest with you. I think of her in past terms, just as Tony is a part of your past. I could be jealous about him, but I know that all that counts in this life is now, the present and nothing else.'

Alex was relieved. It was getting harder to think logically about anything any more, especially as he was closing the gap between them mentally and physically. He surveyed her approvingly before he held out his hand.

'I'm offering you a life with me, Alex. I love you, and I'm hoping that you love me too. I was a bear with a sore head after you left. At some stage Annie realised that I was in love with you. She was the one who encouraged me in no certain terms to sort out the question of an operation or not, and then to find you again, and ask you if you could put up with me for the rest of your life.'

Alex laughed softly. Trust Annie!

'We don't have to live in Charter House. If you want to make a new start somewhere else we will.' His voice was gruff. 'If you tell me that you don't love me, I promise that I'll go away and never bother you again. Just put me out of my misery!'

She reached out and took his hand, carrying it to her cheek. She turned it and kissed the palm. 'For someone who is so intelligent, you certainly reach wrong conclusions and make stupid mistakes sometimes don't you? Of course I love you, you idiot. Or is this visit just a crafty method of getting yourself a gratis assistant for the rest of your life?'

He threw back his head and gave a throaty laugh. His stick clattered to the floor and he pulled her into his arms. His kiss sent the pit of her stomach into a wild swirl. It was a delicious sensation, and raising his mouth from hers, he gazed into her eyes. Burying her face in his neck, she breathed the familiar aftershave, then he kissed her again and she returned his kiss with reckless abandon.

They gazed at each other as emotion whirled and skidded between them.

Finally he exhaled a long sigh of contentment and he managed to sound halfway composed when he asked,

'When will you marry me?'

She felt a warm glow flow through her and felt like laughing out loud in sheer joy. 'Is as soon as possible, soon enough?'

THE END

TROPICAL NIGHTS

Phyllis Humphrey

Tracy Barnes has a few words for real-estate mogul Gregory Thompson. Infuriating. Obstinate. Presumptuous. He's bought the Hawaiian hotel where she works as assistant manager and she could be forced out of her job. If it wasn't for his charm she'd hate him. But Gregory, confident in his ability to win over the guarded Tracy, plans dinner, dancing, and a moonlit walk. Maybe it's Hawaii, but Gregory hasn't felt this good in years . . . or wanted a woman this badly . . .

A MIDSUMMER DREAM

Janet Thomas

Victoria Williams is photographing wildlife on the Cornish cliffs when she meets Bron Macdonald and becomes drawn into his world of filmmaking. During the shooting of an old Cornish legend, Vicky's integrity is threatened by a woman's jealousy. Seemingly insuperable obstacles arise between her and Bron, but are resolved. However, despite their reconciliation, Vicky must choose between loyalty to her sister and her love for Bron. How will she resolve her dilemma? Must she let Bron go?

COLLISION COURSE
WITH LOVE

Sarah Evans

Widowed for over a year, Gabby Balfour decides it's time she moved on. She emigrates to Australia intent on new beginnings, but feels guilty that she's alive while her husband's not. When she meets gorgeous entrepreneur Sam Donovan the attraction is instant, yet she's scared to fall in love again, of being vulnerable and open to the pain of loss. But Sam helps her find closure on her grief and guilt, and the courage to embrace a new love.

LUCREZIA'S SECRET

Toni Anders

In England, Lacey's uncle, a perfumier, wants to re-create Lucrezia Borgia's own perfume. He sends his niece to Capri to obtain the secret formula. Aware of the danger that her mission might be foiled, Lacey fears that there's nobody she can trust — especially when there's a scruffy young man who seems to be stalking her. But when Scott, the helpful Texan, befriends Lacey, will she find that her suspicions about the unkempt and scarily ubiquitous Rob are all wrong?